Stories *for* AIRPORTS

by

Dick Wild

Grosvenor House
Publishing Limited

This book is published by
Grosvenor House Publishing Ltd
Link House
140 The Broadway, Tolworth, Surrey, KT6 7HT.
www.grosvenorhousepublishing.co.uk

A CIP record for this book
is available from the British Library

ISBN 978-1-78623-921-1

Contents

Foreword

As a – now retired – teacher I've been dealing with fiction in one form or another for many years and am constantly on the lookout for short stories that are engaging, relatively quick to read and instantly accessible – in my experience, not so easy to come across as one might imagine.

My approach has always been to address this apparent gap in the market; at times adopting a style close to the traditional fable or folk-tale or veering only slightly from it.

'Airport' fiction has been defined as fiction that might be regarded as 'superficially engaging' whilst not necessarily 'profound or philosophical' (presumably depending on one's interpretation of 'profound' and/or 'philosophical'!)

Nit-picking at such definitions is a pursuit best left to others, other than to conclude the reader's 'engagement' with the story is more likely to be temporary than long-standing and on reading a story, he/she may be inclined to move on...

Which pretty much defines my approach to this – and previous collections: *'Fourteen Shorts'*, *'Sweet & Sour'*, *'Call These Stories'* and *'Telling Tales'*...

At the risk of sounding like one of those writers with a quote for every situation they find themselves in [*see 'The Strange Incident Of The Writer At Night Time'* in the collection *'Telling Tales'*] I think it was J.K. Rowling who said something along the lines of 'someone who doesn't like reading probably hasn't found the right book.' Which I think is a point well made (and one of the few quotes that makes sense to me.) I think it's in all of us to enjoy a tale/story of some description.

How much of all our lives are spent 'telling tales' in some shape or form?

If you aren't an avid reader or may be described as a 'reluctant reader' you may care to give these a try.

If you do – thanks for making the effort.

DW.

Skin

On examining the mail-boxes in the lobby of the building, the two detectives searched for the elevator that would take them to the fifth floor. Both appeared uncharacteristically subdued, their attention devoted to running down a list of names on mail boxes in the lobby before searching for the elevator doors.

On reaching the fifth floor they followed the signs and with an exchange of glances, checked the number and pressed the buzzer.

It took a few seconds for the sound of padded feet to be followed by the door opening, presenting them with their first view of a woman in her early to mid twenties. She had gripped the door like she half expected it to be wrenched from its hinges.

The introductions followed. The woman – Sally Braemore – stared at the IDs and stood aside.

'Is this a homicide enquiry?' she asked.

'No ma'am___'

'Miss.'

'Sorry,' Munroe said.

'I'd assumed it was a homicide enquiry.' She seemed deflated, like being denied involvement in a homicide investigation was something of a disappointment after such a dramatic opening to proceedings.

Having followed her into her living room and watched her perch herself cross-legged on the sofa, the men were eager to get down to business. Taking a seat opposite, Munroe informed her they had some questions relating to a film she'd

1

been involved in the previous year. That there were certain details relating to the film they needed to establish.

If it rang any bells she was giving nothing away – her involvement in the movie business as much a revelation to her as to anyone.

'Movies? I'd assumed it was a burglary or a homicide enquiry. Which is normally the case when detectives come bursting in through your door.'

'I wouldn't say we burst in ma'am.'

'Miss___ No, but you're here all the same.'

Seated opposite permitted a more thorough viewing of the woman they were about to question – whatever preconceived ideas they'd formed proving pretty close to the mark: middish twenties with a frazzle of blonde hair giving way to narrow shoulders and a slim but deceptively shapely figure with jutting breasts protruding visibly into a thin white cotton top.

'Well you don't have to worry on that score ma'am. No-one's been killed.'

'Miss___'

'Sorry...miss.'

'No-one's dead,' Munroe said.

'Yet...' she pointed out, her eyes widening.

'Do you like my apartment?' She looked round, opportunities to be on the receiving end of compliments from detectives bursting through your door in the middle of the afternoon not to be overlooked.

Munroe confirmed it was a 'nice place' as did Sidebottom.

'So – what's this about films?' Sally had adopted her favoured seating position, both feet curled under her but with one leg slightly exposed, allowing a hand to stray and pull at the hem of her skirt.

Munroe steadied his pad on his knee and took hold of his pen. They'd agreed it would be down to him to lead the questioning and for Sidebottom to chip in as and when the occasion demanded. There'd be no arguments from Sidebottom.

Munroe's brief was to keep things simple. To stick to the facts – and remember that, first and foremost, they were detectives simply doing their job.

'We're investigating a piece of film footage that we believe you've been involved in. It went under the title 'Skin' and we believe it was shot in a downtown apartment some time during October last year.' Something clicked.

'Yes,' Sally confirmed. 'That's right.'

'But when we say 'film' we're not talking a full length feature-type movie,' Sidebottom pointed out just to get things straight on that front.

'Oh no,' Sally said, shaking her head. 'It wasn't that kind of film.'

'The film's release is a little complicated in that its distribution is handled by a group who are denying involvement,' Munroe explained. 'What we need to establish is your involvement in that the film – or sequence of film – being released for public viewing, in the presence of fee paying customers___'

'Without a licence__' Sidebottom added.

'As it could point to there being grounds for obscenity.'

'Obscenity! ' Sally's eyes widened.

Munroe was quick to react.

'Which isn't to say the acts themselves were necessarily obscene,' he said.

'I don't think they were at all obscene,' Sally said quickly.

'Well, maybe not. But the point is once that kind of material is made available to public viewing with money changing hands, it becomes a legal issue.' He wasn't entirely sure of the phrase 'that kind of material' but circumstances dictated they were there to do a job and *material* was the word for what they were dealing with here.

'Gee___I knew it was that kind of film, but I didn't know it was *that* kind of film...if you know what I mean. An *obscene* film.'

'Well...' Munroe said. 'That's the way these things tend to be regarded once material of this nature is made available for public viewing.'

'Material'. I never thought of it as 'material' either. But then I'm not a detective.'

Not yet convinced, she pulled the skirt and sank back into the corner of the sofa.

'It never occurred what we were doing was obscene. Sylvy didn't say anything about____'

It was the men's turn to look up.

'This is Sylvester Morrison you're referring to?' Munroe said.

'Yes...Well I don't know...I just knew him as Sylvy.' For the first time she seemed troubled at the prospect of implicating a third party – whatever his role.

'It's okay. We already got the guy tabbed. 'He's down as producer.'

'I don't want to get anyone in trouble,' Sally said.

'No-one's getting anyone in trouble,' Munroe assured her.

'Aside from themselves,' Sidebottom added.

'I like Sylvy,' she said, quickly seeking to make amends for any likely indiscretion. 'I like him a lot.'

'Yes well – I'm sure he's a decent guy,' Sidebottom said.

'He is,' Sally assured them. 'He's a professional. He knows what he's doing and has a way of pushing you to your limits to get the best out of you – as a performer. Which is why he gets such incredible results.'

All of which – true or exaggerated – could wait, the guy's artistic credentials unlikely to feature too majorly in proceedings at this stage.

'What we need to do miss___'

'Sally___'

'Sally...is to run through some of the film's...key-points.'

'The important bits,' Sally said, curling a foot beneath her in readiness to continue. 'Take as long as you like,' she said. 'I'm going nowhere. Are you sure you don't want coffee? Because in the films I've seen the detectives drink lots of coffee.'

'We're fine miss__'

'Sally__'

'We're fine Sally.'

'Good...let me know if you change your mind.'

'We will.'

'Fire away,' she said.

Munroe flicked a page of his note pad and looked up.

'Okay – the film – movie – starts with a man___'

'Bruno,' Sally said.

'Okay, Bruno. Who enters your bedroom from the bathroom completely naked.'

'Completely naked...yes,' Sally confirmed, scratching a point above her knee and recalling the moment. 'I can almost see him standing there now.' The joke – if that's how it was intended – was not lost on Munroe, but would go unacknowledged.

Munroe continued...

'The point being...the man – Bruno – had an erection.'

'Yes he did.' Sally smiled. 'A really powerful one too.' She curled further into the sofa and stared at both men.

'And, I think I'm right in saying that the man – Bruno – then made his way over to the sofa___'

'Yes he did. And he was still extremely erect,' Sally pointed out just to ensure they'd got the details exactly right.

'And then you slipped your dressing-gown from your shoulders and revealed the fact that you were naked too...is that correct?' For convenience he decided to omit the 'completely'.

It appeared to require a moment's thought.

'Yes – that's right. I was stark naked,' she said, her eyes widening. 'Was that obscene?'

Genuine question or not Munroe felt obliged to treat it as such – pointing out that people cavorting together naked either in a bedroom or on a sofa wasn't in itself obscene. Only when it was filmed, and that film got into unlicensed hands for public viewing involving the exchange of money did it get to be an issue...ie. 'obscene'. What people got up to in the privacy of their apartment was their business.

Sally heard the explanation.

'So it isn't so much *what* you do as people *seeing* what you do,' she said.

Munroe thought about it.

'Kind of,' he said.

'Assuming it winds up on film,' Sidebottom pointed out. 'With money exchanging hands...'

Sally was watching Sidebottom who was waiting for Munroe to take them onto the next bit, which as far as Sidebottom was concerned was when things would start to get interesting.

Munroe made a point of checking with his notes.

'Forgive me if I haven't got the next bit exactly right,' he said.

'Don't worry,' Sally assured him, eager for there not to be any misunderstanding in what was after all – a film! It wasn't as if anyone had been murdered.

'The next thing was...you reached out and took the man – Bruno's – erection in your hand!'

'Oh yes, I remember that.' Sally's eyes widened further. 'It seemed the right thing to do with him walking over to me on the sofa – being erect and everything. The way Sylvy put it was...'Just do what comes natural Sally. If it seemed natural to take him in your hand, do it.' So I did.'

She looked at both men.

'Was I wrong to do that?'

'Well___'

'In terms of being obscene I mean___'

'Well miss___'

'Sally.'

'Well Sally____'

'Only in so far that the act was filmed.'

'And the film went public.'

'And money exchanged hands,' Sidebottom explained.

Sally stopped to think about the explanations being put to her.

'Well...I suppose when you put it like that.' She looked at both men.

'I'm sorry,' she said – for the first time sounding genuinely apologetic. 'But it just seemed like the right thing to do. And I did feel something for Bruno. It wasn't simply a question of playing with his cock for the sake of playing with is cock. You understand what I mean by that.'

Both men understood – but it didn't change the facts: that the whole thing had been staged for public viewing.....

'Sylvy told me to imagine I was making a dinosaur's tail out of modelling clay. He was good like that – throwing in bits of advice to make you feel confident about what you were doing, like you were doing something really special; more than just going through the motions with someone pointing a camera at you. Bruno thought it was *really* beautiful. He said it maybe half a dozen times...*Ahh...that's really beautiful honey*."

'Well, like we say...it's once these things get out in the public domain that it gets a little more complicated,' Sidebottom said.

Munroe checked his notes.

'The next thing that happens is...you plant kisses on the man's stomach, until___'

'I kissed him very slowly,' Sally explained. 'The way Sylvy put it was to imagine I was nibbling corn-on-the-cob laced in butter. *Slow Sally...real slow* he would say, so as to get it exactly right.'

'Well miss___'

'Sally.'

'Well Sally' Munroe took a moment, keen to move on but not entirely sure how best to phrase it. 'Correct me if I'm wrong – but we believe you then engaged in oral sex. Is this correct?' 'Oral sex' – he'd thought was the right word. 'Fellatio' was another word but he wasn't sure how you put it...*performed fellatio?...fellated him?* Both sounded a little tacky. The word 'engage' he was less sure about, but maybe it wouldn't matter too much.

Sally had no problem with either word.

7

'Yes,' she said, sinking into the cushion. 'I blew him. I remember that bit. Sylvy was insistent that we got that bit exactly right. Or *I* got the bit exactly right, given I was the one blowing him. He told me to imagine Bruno's cock was a strawberry ice-pole on a hot Summer's day. Which was exactly what I did – exploring every centimetre of him...really slowly.'

She stopped – half expecting the men to put her right on a point or two or maybe break into a round of applause. For some reason neither said a word. She felt a little let down.

'I thought it was really beautiful. So did Bruno. *Beautiful, really beautiful* he was saying. He just kept saying it over and over.'

She stopped again – still half expecting a reaction or maybe wondering if that was the bit that made it obscene.

'Yes well – like we said...it isn't so much *what* you did...'

'As what happened afterwards,' Sidebottom said.

'What – when we fucked?'

'No – afterwards as in____'

'What happened to the film afterwards,' Munroe explained.

'When money exchanged hands,' Sidebottom added.

Sally sighed.

'I took him *very* deep,' she said, crossing her left knee over the right and brushing the curves of both knees. 'But I guess that isn't really the point is it?'

'Not entirely.' Munroe said.

'And then you relax, and the man____'

'Bruno____'

'Yes...Bruno...starts to kiss down your body, whilst you make yourself comfortable in the chair.'

'I looked comfortable – but I wasn't *that* comfortable,' she explained. 'It wasn't easy to look relaxed with Bruno nibbling at me like that, if you can picture what I'm saying. He kissed my breasts. First one, then the other.' She looked down, indicating each tip jutting into the cotton top. 'Right here. But he did it very gently, very sensitively – not like *some* men.' She leant back and smiled. 'It was that kind of film.'

'Then he performed oral sex on you. Is that right?' Munroe said, sufficiently confident to come straight out with it and placing extra stress on the 'you'.

'That's right,' Sally confirmed. 'He licked me. He did it *so* well...beautifully in fact.' She shuffled in her seat. 'Sometimes men aren't so good at doing that.'

She was smiling – accusations along such lines delivered with a smile sufficient to get any man thinking – even detectives.

'Or at least as good as they like to think they are. Maybe if some of them were to watch Bruno doing it they might learn something,' she added, eyeing both men in turn. 'Sylvy said it was one of the most beautiful things he'd ever seen.' Sally hunched herself into the cushion. 'I think he was right.'

Munroe was content to leave it at that. If there was a point where they could afford to relax a little they'd probably reached it. What followed would be relatively straightforward, almost routine in contemporary cinematic terms.

'Then you had sexual intercourse. Is that right?' Munroe was confident this was definitely the right word given there weren't many other words to choose from (that would stand up in court.) There was nothing particularly controversial, or 'obscene' about intercourse. Intercourse was how babies were made.

Sally wasn't so sure.

'Well – Bruno fucked me on the sofa if that's what you mean. He was on top. I was underneath...at first. It was beautiful. Do you mind if I smoke?' There were no objections.

She reached for a pack of cigarettes on the table. 'Bruno really knew how to screw; how to please a woman. Which is more than can be said for *some* men.'

She drew a cigarette from the packet and curled her lips round the filter. The detectives watched as she reached to the table for a lighter.

'One of my few vices,' she said, indicating the freshly lit cigarette and readying herself to continue.

'Bruno being on top was correct...at first. But then we switched, and I went on top, so it was like me fucking Bruno instead of Bruno fucking me.' She was holding the cigarette at a distance by way of illustration. 'Sylvy insisted we did it that way so as to show a woman in a position of control.' She tipped the ash in the tray. 'It was that kind of film. I'd struggle to see how anyone could say a woman being shown in a position of control was obscene.'

She rolled the cigarette, half expecting one of them – most likely Sidebottom – to step in and explain it to her. 'I'd say that position was pretty common these days. Though maybe not so much with older people.' Not for the first time she had both men firmly in her sights.

If she was looking for a reaction she'd likely have to wait. But for now it wasn't really the point. Maybe it was the circumstances that awarded her a distinct feeling of being in charge; that they may be detectives, but she was the one dictating proceedings – providing the information.

'We didn't finish like that,' she said, having got them thus far feeling obliged to complete the picture. 'He finished on my tummy.' She rotated a hand above her waist with the fingers spread. 'Which I thought was...kind of cute.'

Which, appropriately perhaps, was the cue to bring pro-ceedings to a halt. All that remained – to take her through some details on the contractual side – with or without the involvement of Sylvester Morrison, including her fee and the terms under which it was negotiated.

It was on issuing a statement confirming they had no further questions for now but that if anything should spring to mind she should contact the number on the card and ask for detectives Munroe or Sidebottom, that she eased forwards and for the first time reached to make contact with the closer of the two detectives. Maybe it was seeing their names handed to her in black and white. She stared as the card exchanged hands, a hand coming to rest lightly on Munroe's arm – thoughts of films and all references to them temporarily put to one side.

'Am I going to prison?' There was unease in the voice, mindful that the men were after all detectives investigating criminal activity. And despite having done her bit – answering each question as honestly and openly as would be expected – all indications pointed to there being more to come. She watched the two men rise from their seats.

'It just seems odd – the idea of going to prison for doing something that, at the time, seemed really beautiful.'

Both men stopped before making their exit.

'I'd say it's unlikely,' Munroe said. 'The law tends to come down more heavily on those behind these operations.'

'Those responsible for releasing the footage for public viewing,' Sidebottom explained.

Sally was listening. *Released footage...public viewing...*It all seemed a million miles from an afternoon spent fucking with Bruno – on or off camera.

'It's strange,' she said, a hand still lingering close to the two detectives now stood by the door. 'To think that it's not so much *what* you do as people *seeing* what you do.' She looked at the two men. 'Next time I'm watching a movie with people dying and kids getting shot I'll remind myself that what I'm seeing is no way near as obscene as two people fucking in someone's apartment.'

The men buttoned coats and turned to the door.

'But then I'm not a detective.'

Making their way through the door Munroe explained they'd be in contact depending how things went with legal representation – adding they could arrange for someone to act on her behalf if she so wished. She thought about it briefly, concluding Sylvy would be the one to deal with that kind of thing. After all, he was the brains behind the operation.

'Thank you miss,' Sidebottom said, turning to leave.

'You've been very helpful,' Munroe added.

'That's okay,' Sally said, holding the door open like she half expected it to be wrenched off its hinges. The men stepped through it and out onto the corridor.

'I hope I don't go to prison,' she said finally, watching the men turn to leave.

'We'll do what we can,' Munroe said.

Both men made their way to the elevator door where they stopped, waiting for the red indicator light to rise from the lobby. Sidebottom turned to Munroe.

'What do you think?'

Munroe waited for the doors to open.

'I thought it was beautiful,' he said, stepping forwards. 'How about you?'

Sidebottom stepped into the space making room for Munroe.

'I think I need to speak to my wife,' he said.

The door closed.

* * * *

The Cab Driver's Tale

It was the end of Jinsky's shift, the latest in a line of graveyard shifts that Jinsky was convinced had been dumped on him on account of him being Polish – or East European, or simply non-American. He had no way of proving it, it was just a hunch, but a hunch he found reassuring at the end of his shift when he was left to remove all manner of unsightly debris left as souvenirs on his rear seat every 'goddamned' night of the week.

The coffee-bar on the corner of the station was busier than usual. Taking his place at the counter he took a look over his shoulder.

The guys were already in place – each armed with his own moment of amusement, observation, experience – designed to kill a little time, raise a laugh or two, or at least be as amusing as the guy who spoke before you.

Jinsky stood a moment and then turned to head for the table. There were times when he'd have preferred to head for a different table but not having been on this team that long he knew there were rules designed to make life a little easier for everyone, and that opting to sit at a different table at the end of the graveyard shift was not one of them.

'Jinsky!' As ever, the exclamation – though little more than acknowledgment of his arrival – was announced in such a way to make it a big event.

There was a shifting of seats to let Jinsky slot into place. Another rule – allowing whoever was speaking to get to the end of his tale without interruption. Jinski's arrival – big event though it was at the time – was instantly forgotten.

Al was in the chair.

'So I said to the guy. I don't know or care about how you're going to get the thing home. No way you're gonna bring that Goddamn thing in the cab. So the guy's standing there holding this basket up against the window, looking into it and pointing at the snake's head peering through at the glass. 'Fuck you' he says. 'You ain't nothing but a big fat snake yourself'! Laughter followed. Al readied himself to continue.

'Then he goes and calls another cab like he's set on hauling this fucking six foot snake round town like some fucking zoo-keeper.'

'Or circus-tamer...'

'Or a cab-driver – with a taste for the exotic.'

'Sounds like a job for you Rocco. I hear all Italians, especially the girls, have a taste for the exotic.'

'Especially the Sicilians.'

Rocco was saying nothing.

Though commonly referred to as Italian, Rocco wasn't Italian, he was Sicilian – a trifling distinction to immigration officials who had little inclination to spend their time pinning donkeys' tails on places they'd never even heard of. Rocco too had his tales to tell – none of which were to be wasted on a bunch of deadbeats sitting round a table at the end of a night-shift.

Still content to view proceedings from a distance Jinsky eased into his seat. Being the newest on the team, as well as Polish, meant there were other rules to stick to. Less obligation to speak but when you *did*, to make sure it got a laugh. There was nothing more irritating than a guy who rarely spoke telling a tale that wasn't even remotely funny. Which was fine by Jinsky. Out of necessity he'd been a keen student of the language since arriving on these shores. Aided by being an excellent listener. And sitting with a bunch of wise-cracking guys at four in the morning was as good a place to start as any.

Cindy arrived bearing cups of coffee, making space with a free hand to unload the cups.

'I hear they just voted you the best waitress in town Cindy.'

'And I heard you say that to every waitress.' Cindy too knew there were certain rules to stick to, having an answer for every cab-driver without a home to go to being first on the list.

'Only the ones called Cindy,' Cy said, shifting closer and looking over his shoulder.

Taking one of the cups, it was Hughie's turn to speak.

'I had a guy yesterday dressed in a clown's uniform. I'm thinking he's going to tell me to take him to some circus or to some kids' party. But he just climbs into his seat and tells me his mom's been taken sick and he needs to get home soon and to step on it. So why the clown outfit?'

'Maybe his mom figures he's a funny guy and likes him to dress the part.'

'You should have told him a joke,' said Al.

'The one about the clown who finds his girl in bed with a Roman soldier and turns to the guy and says...he was *glad-e-ate-her.*'

Jinsky took a bite of his sandwich, turning it once and then once again for closer examination.

'Meat a little spicy for you Jinsky?' Al had his eye on the others as he spoke.

'You should try an Italian sausage,' said Hughie, eyeing Rocco.

'As The Pope said to the actress,' said Stu.

'Talking of the Pope, one time I had a priest and a nun together. Same fare, same cab.' Al turned his attention to a second can of beer.

'Lapsed Catholics,' said Stu.

'Said not to tell a soul,' said Hughie.

'Lest The Pope found out.'

'Or his wife...'

'Those guys don't have wives...'

'Okay – his mother.'

Al took two mouthfuls of beer from the can as Stu turned to face Rocco.

'How 'bout you Rocco? You picked up anyone famous since we last met?'

'Like The Pope?'

'Or a clown dressed as The Pope?'

'Or a priest?'

'Or a priest dressed as a clown?'

'Disguised as a clown so no-one would tell The Pope.'

'Or his wife...'

'Or his mother...'

Rocco took a fistful of potato chips from a packet.

'Yeh – I picked up a guy asked me why I came to America.'

Cy looked round, grinning in anticipation of what was assumed would be a worthy punch-line.

'So what d' you tell him Rocco?'

'To get laid and drink beer,' said Hughie.

'Which is not so easy to do in Italy.'

'Least not at the same time,' said Al

'Or in Sicily,' said Stu.

'Or anywhere where it gets too hot,' said Al.

Rocco took a potato chip, turning it once or twice in his fingers.

'I told him my people came here for two reasons: to make a new life, to bring up my children up good and decent___'

'And Catholic...' Al interjected.

'But – more important than that.' Rocco wanted to be seen ignoring the interruption. 'Because of the sense of humour.'

'That's three reasons,' said Hughie.

'Did the guy laugh?'

'Yeh, he thought it was real funny.'

'Well – that's America for you.'

Eyes turned to where Jinsky continued to rotate what remained of his sandwich before looking back across the table.

'How 'bout you Jinsky?' They got cabs in Poland?'

'Or cab drivers with a sense of humour?'

'Yeh – they got a flat rate fare; anywhere you want to go, same price,' said Hughie.

Jinsky took a napkin and folded it meticulously like he was about to perform a ceremony at the altar.

'Yeh – they got cabs,' he said.

'Got drivers too,' said Al.

'Too may drivers,' said Stu. 'That's why they all get sent over here.'

'To make it one big happy family,' said Sammy.

'Cept for the Italians.'

'And the Sicilians.'

Like the sign above the door said, or *used* to say before it got subjected to a little off-the-cuff alteration – they *were* just one big happy family!

'So Jinsky – you pick up any nice little Polish girls tonight once the bars closed?'

'Someone a little exotic?'

'Like an Italian?'

'Or a Sicilian.'

Jinsky turned the napkin slowly in his other hand.

'No Polish girls, not today,' he said. 'Maybe tomorrow.'

'Well you know what they say...What's good's worth waiting for.'

He put what remained of his sandwich on the plate and began a methodical wiping of his mouth.

'I got one guy though. Interesting guy. Gets in the cab and after two or three blocks calls from the back, leaning forward like he needs to know I'm listening.'

Having done with the napkin he laid it to rest on the table. Jinsky always found it easier to speak when he had nothing to distract him.

'The man said he was going to let me into a secret. His voice is low – like in one of those films. First – he tells me his wife is sleeping with other men. And I'm thinking why is this guy telling me his wife's sleeping with other men? What he says is...he happens to know that two of the guys sleeping with his wife, or 'fucking his wife'... that was the way the man put it – are cab drivers working in this part of the city. Would you believe that? Then he moves closer. And I'm thinking he's gonna pull a gun and blow my fuckin' brains out – like he thinks I'm one of the guys! But what he says is he happens to know who the two guys are – that he's got their names and knows everything about them: where they live, where they work. And that any day now he's gonna pay them a visit with a .38 and leave their brains smeared over the windscreen of their cabs, or maybe on the street, whichever comes first.. That's the way he said it – just like that!'

Jinsky nudge the discarded napkin to one side and brushed his lips.

'I think my English is getting pretty good,' he added, smiling. 'What do you guys think?'

Steve split what remained of the bag of chips and laid it on the table. Al took a mouthful of beer and pushed the half empty can to one side.

'I think some guys got no sense of humour,' he said.

Oddly no-one was laughing.

* * * * *

The Comfort-Zone

It was on a typically blustery April day that a man in his early forties dressed in full regalia of ankle length coat and hat to match descended the steps of his brownstone tenement. As ever, his aim first and foremost – to take a little air, clear his head from the clutter of his apartment for an hour or two and if anything beyond that were to turn up – then so be it.

Pausing to light a Winston, he set off on a familiar route taking him two blocks to the entrance to the northernmost part of the park, always a popular retreat for the city's uptown inhabitants: the pathways, lawns and trees – at this time of year already showing signs of blossom – a welcome contrast to the grey bustling streets beyond the park's perimeter.

Strolling alongside the quarter mile or so of flower beds and tennis-courts he reached an arrangement of gardens that had become something of a second home during his afternoon strolls – an area comprising two rectangular lawns separated by paths and surrounded by bushes, a few benches and rows of plants already close to full bloom. In short: an ideal spot to rest one's feet for an hour or two, take stock of one's thoughts, or in his case – take up a position on a nearside corner, light a second cigarette and take in the area fanning out toward a line of trees and the entrance kiosk for the tennis-courts.

It was on completing his perusal of the scene that his eye fell on a youngish woman seated on the bench not far from where he was standing: a woman evidently in the throes of some deep meditation, and even from this vantage point – blessed with quite handsome features, albeit currently concealed behind hands held in a semi-bowed, praying kind of pose. Occasionally she would lift her head, directing her attention towards a small section of the flower-bed beyond the path as if something intensely precious was hidden there – within vision yet frustratingly beyond reach.

The man stood a while, not wishing to be seen as encroaching but prepared to take in a little more of the woman's moment of vigil.

Watching as – at that very moment – the woman straightened herself in her seat – her thoughts, tears or whatever had commanded her attention – temporarily put to one side in order to tend to something in her bag.

It was whilst delving into her bag that her eye happened to fall on the figure clad in coat and hat, looking unobtrusively in her direction. Bystanders being far from a rarity in what was, after all, a public place, she had no problem with the likelihood of her being observed.

Equally – the man had few qualms about standing his ground. He stubbed the cigarette into the tarmac and made a point of walking casually towards the seat – vindicated in it being the only seating space available along this particular stretch of path.

Whatever the source of the woman's discontent, it had little impact on her features: fine nose, a delicate mouth drawn some way between a frown and a smile and eyes that shone in part, but with a glazed, distant look about them. It was shortly after taking his seat that she acknowledged his presence with a small smile, and with time on her side, felt obliged to offer some sort of explanation.

'It's my husband,' she said, her eyes instantly back to the floral display beyond the path. 'The authorities offered me a slot which I thought was a nice gesture.' He nodded whilst searching for something concealed in his top pocket.

'He worked for the city,' she said. 'Parks And Recreation Department.' It was followed by a further wiping of an area just above her top lip, brushing what remained of a tear from her cheek and putting the tissue to one side.

'You can see it there from where I'm sitting,' she said. Whether an invitation to share a closer view he couldn't be sure, but there was little reason to assume otherwise: shifting only slightly so as not to come across as being too intrusive. He spotted a small metal plate surrounded by a bed of tiny pink blue and red flowers.

'Nice touch,' he said, hands slotted in his pockets before returning to an upright position.

'I like this spot.' She eyed lines of distant figures each immersed in their own private worlds. 'Chance to lose your-self...chance to think...'

The man concurred; certainly the ideal spot for a moment's quiet reflection.

'It's good to talk,' he said.

'And there are times when it's good to listen.'

Indication of which was an arm descending from the rear of the seat – an invitation to step across and join her – a gesture that would be imprudent to ignore.

He followed her across the path where she knelt to brush a few impediments from the area surrounding the small slate panel screwed to a wooden plate, then taking the tissue she'd screwed into a ball to wipe across its surface.

'It was either this or an inscription on a seat in one of the council chambers,' she said, tending to a few sweeps of the soil before accompanying him back to their seats. Not a difficult decision.

'You must think I'm a little crazy,' she said, her eyes lowered to fingers fumbling in her lap.

'Only a little,' he said.

It was with that sense of time – or events – catching up on you, that he suggested he accompany her back to her apartment in a taxi he'd be happy to pay for, the streets immediately beyond the park's vicinity being none too inviting for a single woman following an afternoon stroll in the park. She appeared to hold back a moment, her eye back to the plaque only feet away – aware it was an offer she'd be foolish to dismiss out of hand, particularly as she still found the prospect of arriving home alone a little difficult to cope with.

Once on their feet they retraced their steps alongside the lines of tennis-courts, stepping up the pace only once beyond the park gates in order to attract the attention of a cab. Eventually having one draw up and minutes later take the fare that had brought them to the entrance to the woman's apartment block.

It was stepping from the cab and reaching for his arm that first brought them into contact.

'I think we could both use a coffee,' she said, observing the formalities reach completion through the cab driver's window.

He let her lead the way, following the elegant stride step by step. It was only the third floor so there was little need to use the elevator. She'd never been keen on using elevators.

It was a modest apartment, tastefully furnished but without losing its homely feel. She made for the kitchen and he followed, waiting, standing in the doorway watching her spoon coffee and in the artificial light from above, looking even paler than in the park. He made his way to her side and took the cup she was offering in one hand.

He had removed his hat and coat and before taking his seat crossed the room to the window. He liked to view the city at this time of day: the sidewalks finding a renewed lease of life, lights rapidly spreading from street to street like any city in the midst of celebration.

She sidled up to him, the cup gripped tightly in one hand, following him to the sofa.

Once seated – aware of his presence as if for the first time – she allowed herself to be drawn into the crook of his shoulder, touched by the sensation of male company, the feel of a bristled chin nudging against her cheek. And seconds later, the feel of warm lips brushing her neck, fingers flicking at the collar of her top, loosened to expose an entire length of collar-bone.

Whether anticipating how she'd react, she couldn't be sure. But it came from somewhere – an instant rising to her feet to make her way to the window, where she stopped, looking back over her shoulder.

'I'm sorry,' she said. 'You probably think I'm crazy.'

The second time she'd made the observation. And for the second time, getting the same response.

'Only a little,' he said.

She watched him reach for his coffee, downing its contents and reaching for his hat.

'I guess I still need more time,' she said quickly, hesitating to make the point yet still feeling it needed to be said.

'It's okay,' he said, reaching for his coat and drawing it over his shoulders.

'Maybe next time,' she said, moving to the door to oversee his departure with hopefully some saving of face.

'Yes – maybe next time,' he said. With his hat firmly back in place, he stepped to the door to make his exit.

It was some days later that a man in full April regalia was seen descending the steps from his apartment – setting off on what was, by now, a familiar route – taking him to the entrance and then on to the northwest corner of the park, where – on reaching his favoured spot – he lit a second cigarette and took in the area fanning out toward a line of trees and the entrance kiosk for the tennis-courts.

It was on completing his perusal of the scene that his eye fell on a woman in the throes of some deep meditation.

He stubbed the cigarette into the tarmac and made a point of sauntering casually over to the seat vindicated in it being the only seat along this particular stretch of path.

The woman looked up.

'It's my husband,' she said. 'He worked for the Parks And Recreation Department'.

The man nodded whilst appearing to search for something concealed in his top pocket....

* * * * *

When Margarita
Met Candice

[A sequel to 'Margarita'...'Margarita-Mark-Two'...and
'Satisfaction'...stories featured in previous anthologies: '*Call
These Stories*'...and '*Telling Tales*']

It's been different, there's no denying that, but you get used to
things in time and things have been going okay since my wife
left. I'm getting better at cooking and sometimes put meat in
the oven because it tends to stick to the pan on the electric
ring. Candice is still with me. Though she doesn't say much it's
quite nice having her around. I decided to buy her some
clothes instead of giving her my wife's old stuff to wear
because in a way it didn't seem right doing that. After all, it's
because of Candice that my wife left. But that's in the past.
The best thing to do when things like that happen is to look
to the future.

We got into a kind of routine. I'd go to work and come
home, we'd have tea and watch tv, maybe have a glass of wine
or a cup of cocoa later on; then off to bed. A good thing about
Candice is we can make love as many times a week as we
want. With my wife it was twice a week. I think this might be
because I didn't satisfy her. She told me as much one night
because she thought I ought to know so it wasn't me imagining
it or her making it up. That's how me and Candice got
together. I got Candice from town to practise on so I could
satisfy my wife, but my wife caught me practising on her when
she came home from yoga early and got the wrong idea. She
screamed and then started sobbing and wouldn't talk to me,

until the morning when she *did* talk to me, but only to tell me she was leaving. Which looking back on it I thought was a bit unfair. Candice was a plastic doll not a woman and I was only practising on her because I wasn't satisfying my wife, so in a way she was the one who started it. But she didn't seem to be in the mood for listening, so I didn't say anything except to ask when she was coming back. She said she didn't know if she was *ever* coming back, which proved to be the case.

It was all a bit unfortunate, but – it's another story and now I'm kind of used to Candice and things are going okay. It's odd to think how failing to satisfy my wife could have such a big effect on my life. Sometimes – when I'm making love to Candice I wonder if she's being satisfied but it's difficult to say – her eyes and mouth are wide open which makes it look as if she's being satisfied, but they're nearly always open and because she doesn't say much it's difficult to be sure. But – and this is another point...maybe it doesn't really matter. I sometimes ask myself if I'm being satisfied when I make love to Candice, and it's difficult to be absolutely sure. I think mostly I am, which is the main thing. At first there were times when I imagined Candice was my wife when we were making love but it seemed a strange thing to be thinking so I stopped doing it. I thought about telling my wife that when she told me she was leaving, but looking back I think it might have made things worse.

It was some time after my wife and I had split up that I had a mind to venture outside with Candice. Being cooped up indoors all day long isn't ideal for anyone. She didn't say anything but I thought I detected a glint in her eye at the prospect of leaving the house for a while. I put her in a blue plaited skirt I'd bought her the previous week so she'd look a bit of an eye-catcher even though we were only going for a stroll, but I know women, particularly younger women, like to look that way and I didn't want her to feel I was letting her down.

We went for a walk in the park. It was fairly warm but there was a breeze blowing that stopped us getting too hot. People looked and one or two smiled which was nice. One or two were laughing, but being in the park on a warm afternoon can make you feel like laughing. After a while it got a bit tricky walking arm in arm so I decided that next time we went out we'd go somewhere to sit down. There are cafes you can go to but I'm not keen on cafes because they tend to be a bit cramped and I usually drink my coffee and eat my muffin too quickly and no sooner have I sat down than I'm ready to get up and go. I prefer to sit in a pub. I used to go to the pub occasionally with my wife, but it had to be a nice pub because some pubs could be smoky and noisy. But now you can't smoke in pubs or cafes so it isn't an issue. She used to tell me off for smoking in bed because the smell lingers. But now she's gone I can smoke as many cigarettes in bed as I like. I like to smoke cigarettes because it helps me think.

So next time we went out we went to a pub in town. It's the only pub in town that seems okay inside. The others are a bit depressing, mainly men sitting at the bar looking fed up. I decided to go fairly early when it was quiet. I don't like it when pubs get busy.

There weren't many people around when we went in. The barman was washing a glass. He was in a good mood, or seemed in a good mood – when he saw me and Candice he laughed and then used the f word. I wasn't quite sure why he used the f word and was thinking it was a good thing I wasn't with my wife because she hated hearing the f word and thinks it's appalling that people use such words. I think it's more appalling when people – particularly babies – die of starvation, but you can't always talk about these things with your wife. Candice barely blinked an eyelid. I occasionally use the f word, but only when it slips out like if I stub my toe or bang my knee on the corner of a cupboard. And – when we're making love. When we make love we both like to use the f word; Candice says it a lot, other words too, and sometimes the c word – which, in bed, I don't mind. It's different when you're making love and sometimes these words help me time my thrusts, which is one of the things we learnt at Mave's class on 'satisfying your wife in bed'.

Anyway, I helped Candice onto her seat at the bar. Fortunately there was a stool with a back which stopped her toppling off. The barman asked me what I wanted to drink so I said I'd have a pint of Best Bitter, and a vodka and orange for Candice. He used the f word again and tittered. He seemed to like using the f word, which is something a lot of men like to do in pubs.

Although it shouldn't really matter, it felt good being in the pub with Candice because she's quite pretty. She's certainly prettier than my wife, which isn't saying a great deal because my wife isn't particularly pretty, or at least she wasn't when she was with me. She's what you'd call 'ordinary' looking – like me. In fact I sometimes wonder if that was one of the reasons she left – because Candice is prettier. Who knows? It's difficult to be sure about these things and probably best not to think about them too much.

The barman put a pint of beer in front of me 'And a vodka for the missus.' I didn't bother telling him we weren't married because there didn't seem much point and it wouldn't have made any difference to the cost.

I pointed a few things out to Candice: the football flags on the wall, the CD player and the stack of papers in a rack. The barman was amused and sharing a joke with a few of the men at the bar, which is something men do in pubs, so I kind of chuckled along when one of them caught my eye. One of them was trying to get Candice's eye which I didn't think was quite right. You shouldn't go making eyes at women in pubs because it looks as if you're after them. They call it flirting and means you want to have sex with them later, but with some men it can go a bit too far.

I drank my beer and ordered a packet of dry roasted nuts.

'Anything for the lady?' the barman asked, looking at his mates. I told him Candice wouldn't want anything to eat. Then he laughed again and so did the other men.

The tv was on but I don't like watching tv in a pub. You can't hear what is being said and the picture isn't always clear.

I talked to Candice, pointing out how the froth of the beer sticking to the glass is a good sign and meant I might have another pint of the same beer instead of trying a different one. Candice looked a picture – sitting there bolt upright in her seat in her nice new plaited skirt with her mouth open like she was about to break into song which can sometimes happen in pubs. I helped her out with her drink as she isn't a big drinker. I didn't like it much but they don't like it if you sit in the pub without a drink in front of you.

The men at the end of the bar had been watching us and grinning. I think maybe they were a bit jealous because Candice is quite pretty with big eyelashes and freckles. Or they might have been looking at her breasts which are not big but stick out a bit like the tips of ice-cream cones. They shouldn't really have been looking at her breasts like that but it's another thing men like to do in pubs and then talk to each other about it.

It was shortly after that one of the men who had very little hair and a burly face came up and leant on the bar next to us. He was smiling and looking at his friends and then he asked if I was 'all right.' I said 'yes' and then he was looking at Candice. I didn't know if he was looking at her breasts or her face but it didn't seem to matter much, maybe it was both. He was grinning and looking at his friends and then he looked back and said…

'How's your missus?' The other men turned away. I didn't bother telling him me and Candice weren't married, which is what men usually mean when they call a woman your missus – because I didn't think it really mattered and I didn't think he would have been interested. He was still grinning and looking at his mates so I looked and grinned too to be friendly which made them grin even more and start laughing all over again.

He looked back at Candice and asked a rude question which I wasn't surprised to hear him ask because he looked the type to ask those sorts of questions. He asked if I was having sex with Candice, though he didn't say it like that.

He said... 'Are you giving her one?' which I've heard men say when they mean having sex. His mates were laughing even more. It's strange how a lot of men laugh at these sorts of things. Anyway I didn't think it was the sort of question he should be asking so I didn't say anything. I just took another handful of peanuts and another drink of beer. But he was smiling and asked me if I was deaf and I said 'no', and he asked if I'd heard the question. I said 'yes' and he asked me the same question again. I thought it might be best to answer him instead of saying nothing, so I told him me and Candice were in a relationship, but I didn't say more because I didn't think it was any of his business. He was amused and bent over the bar laughing with his mates. They all seemed to be happy about hearing me and Candice were in a relationship which is quite a jolly thing to hear about so I laughed along too for a few seconds which seemed to get everyone in a happy frame of mind.

Despite the laughter I was hoping the man would leave us but he just leant back against the bar and ordered more pints of lager for him and his friends. I got the impression he was thinking of another question he could ask me or Candice. I wondered about offering him a peanut but decided against because he might see it as an invitation to stay longer. He was still looking at his mates and then he looked at Candice and said she'd got nice breasts. He didn't actually use the word 'breasts' he said 'tits' which is another word for breasts. I said 'thankyou' because it's a kind of compliment and he was right, and maybe I'd been right when I'd wondered if they were looking at her breasts earlier.

He then said she didn't say much, which was true and for a moment I thought he might be about to reach out and squeeze one of Candice's breasts so she might say something, which is where I would have had to step in and say 'No you can't do that.' Because going up to women in pubs and squeezing their breasts is something you shouldn't do, nor is it the sort of thing you should want to do. Just because a woman has nice breasts doesn't mean you can go up to her and start squeezing them.

I said 'no' when he commented on Candice not saying much, explaining that she wasn't really one for conversation. He grinned and looked at the barman who was scowling a bit and then leant forward to say something in his ear. I think he might have told him not to say those sorts of things about Candice's breasts because when you run a pub you have to careful about what men say sometimes.

Anyway the man went back to his mates. One of them looked at me and held his arm at a right-angle at the elbow and jerked it upwards like he was lifting weights.

I finished my beer and ordered another one. I didn't get Candice another drink as there was still plenty left in her glass, and like I say, she isn't a big drinker. I sat on the stool next to Candice and for a while it was nice – sitting there passing time drinking beer and eating peanuts. The men had quietened down a bit and didn't seem to be looking at Candice as much. Maybe knowing she was spoken for meant there was little to be gained from it.

I toyed with having a third pint and said 'Why not? You only live once.'

I decided to try a different beer which was lighter and a bit more bitter. I smacked my lips and offered Candice a drink – but only jokingly. She'd barely touched her vodka.

It was as I was taking another drink that I was aware of someone not far away watching us – a man who'd just arrived and seemed to be about the same age as me sitting at a nearby table and drinking slowly. At first I thought it was just me he was looking at but it was obviously Candice too, in fact mainly Candice, which had me thinking maybe he was after her, which meant I had to be on my guard.

When he came up and stood by me I was ready to tell him Candice was mine and he should respect that. But he didn't say anything for a bit, just stood there sipping his drink. I wondered why he'd left his table if he was just going to stand there. It was soon after that he asked after Candice. I told him her name and he nodded and said she was a fine figure of a woman. Which was maybe right. He then said that he had a similar partner and her name was Margarita. I said 'Oh really?' and he said 'Yes.'

He pulled up a stool and we got talking. I wondered if he was telling fibs but he seemed to be sincere about it, telling me how he'd got his partner from a shop in town, which was interesting because that's where I'd got Candice after Mave's class. He asked about Mave's class. I told him it's where you go if you can't satisfy your wife in bed. But my wife had caught me practising on Candice and the following morning walked out. I said I didn't think it was fair and he agreed. He said that's the way it goes some times, which is a good way of putting it and I think he's right. He was interested in Candice and said she had a few more freckles than Margarita and her mouth was more open. I said I didn't really know why her mouth was open all the time because we didn't often talk and Candice hardly ever said a word. He said it was to do with 'variety being the spice of life' saying it in a joking way and winking. I didn't really understand what he meant but I didn't bother asking him.

Anyway we talked a little more and he suggested next time he could bring Margarita along. Like Candice, she didn't get out a lot and it would make a change and it would be company for them too. I thought this was a good idea and told him so. I was interested to meet Margarita. So we agreed that in four days time we'd meet in the same place at the same time.

When the day came I walked to the pub with Candice on my arm which I noticed got quite a few admiring looks. Like I say, Candice is nice looking and I'm not surprised people like looking at her.

Me and Candice got to the pub first. Sitting Candice on the same stool as before I noticed the men in the corner were the same men as before and were looking across and nudging each other. I was thinking maybe they had their eye on Candice because men in pubs like to eye women, particularly if they're fetching-looking in a blue dress and yellow top. The barman remembered us from last time and was smiling and looking at the men as he pulled the beer and put the glass under the vodka bottle.

'Ice?' he asked, looking over his shoulder and still laughing. I nodded and took some money out of my wallet.

'All right darling?' one of the men called across. I looked across but I didn't say anything because it was likely Candice he was talking to rather than me.

When the man arrived with Margarita it caused something of a stir. The men were almost beside themselves and the barman used the f word again and shook his head.

He introduced Margarita and I shook her hand and he put her on a stool next to Candice so they could chat together like women do in pubs. I asked about getting her a drink but it was difficult to hear anything with the men laughing at the end of the bar. I think one of them must have said a funny joke. I ordered a beer and a gin and tonic and we all took our seats.

Candice and Margarita were similar looking; almost like sisters: slightly puffed-out cheeks and freckles and big round eyes, and she too had her mouth open – the pair sitting there looking like they'd been chatting away together for hours.

We took turns telling each other how we'd met and it was interesting how our stories were similar, it might even have been the same place in town though I can't remember it too well now. He told me about his last Margarita who he'd carelessly burnt with a cigarette after a sex-session which was very unfortunate.

'Picture it,' he said, standing for a moment and leaning against the bar. 'One minute making love, the next – seeing her wither to nothing on my sofa.' He shook his head and said he'd had to go outside and have another cigarette. I said I could see his point. If it had happened to me I'd have had to smoke a cigarette too because smoking cigarettes helps me think. I shook my head. He said it's funny how things can turn out the way you least expect, and I agreed.

I told him how Candice had come on the scene: how I'd got her to practise on so I could satisfy my wife; only she'd come home early from yoga and caught us, which was also a bit unfortunate and he nodded and said he remembered me telling him last time. I told him how my wife had cried and screamed, though not in that order. She'd actually screamed before she had cried. And the next thing she had walked out and hadn't come back. I shook my head and the man – whose name was Thomas – rolled his eyes, took another drink of beer and said 'That's women for you.' Which in a way is right and I nodded and took another drink too and asked him if he wanted a peanut and he said yes and opened his hands so I gave him a few instead of just one.

We got onto talking about our 'sex-sessions' as Thomas liked to call them, which is the kind of thing men talk about in pubs and with Candice and Margarita chatting away a few feet away it wouldn't be a problem. Thomas shifted a bit closer and said how he liked Margarita to go 'on top' and asked if I'd ever tried that with Candice. I seemed to remember there being something on the last page of Mave's booklet about things like that. *Variety is the spice of love* I think it said at the top of the page. I said how having Candice on top would likely help me with my thrusts which is important when you're trying to satisfy a woman. He moved closer still and told me about taking her doggy-style and giving her 'a bit of a spanking' which I thought was an interesting idea though I wasn't entirely sure what he meant by the 'doggy-style' bit. I looked across imagining giving Candice a bit of a spanking and her turning to me and asking why I was giving her a spanking and me telling her it was to do with 'timing my thrusts'. All of which goes to show there's more to the business of making-love than many people realise.

We were well into our second beers now and it's sometimes easier to talk about these when you've had a few beers. He was laughing when he shifted closer again and told me about *Hooray Henry* which from the way he described it is a plastic prong that he got from the same shop as Margarita who had actually taken quite a shine to it. He told me how it worked and I was thinking it would be a good idea for a Christmas present for Candice. Buying your partner presents at Christmas isn't always easy and this would be good idea because it wouldn't be too big and I quite liked the idea of showing her how it worked once it had been unwrapped.

It was whilst we were talking that I noticed two of the men from the end of the bar had come across to stand next to Margarita and Candice. They were laughing and looking back at their friends and nudging each other like they were trying to make each other fall over.

'All right darlin'?' one was saying. Me and Thomas looked at each other and then looked at the bar to give the impression we didn't want to talk to them.

' 'Right mate?' One said to either me or to Thomas and I raised a hand. I wasn't sure about saying anything because you're never sure how things like that will develop with men in pubs. They were asking about their names and Thomas told them. They laughed and asked if they ever did a lesbo-act. I laughed a bit too because it seemed like the best thing to do though I wasn't quite sure what they meant. Anyway the barman came up and said something to them and I think he might have told them to cool it which seemed like a good idea. Like last time it was likely they were just flirting with them which can happen in pubs but it wasn't really the right thing to do because they were spoken for. And maybe they could see his point because they went back to their mates who thumped them on the shoulders and shook their heads.

Thomas rolled his eyes at me and I did the same back. One of the men looked across and stood up saying 'If you want a real man darlin' come and take a ride on this.' I'm not sure who he was talking to but I thought it was likely Candice or Margarita.

There were other people in the pub by now sitting at tables and looking across. Some were talking in whispers and pointing in our direction. I think maybe they'd been hearing what the men had been saying and were telling each other how it was wrong and if men like them wanted a woman they should get their own instead of trying to get someone else's.

Thomas ordered more beer and told me about when they'd once visited Shrewsbury to see his parents in the pub they go to after church. How he didn't get on with them too well, not having married or had a family or a proper job or a nice house to live in with a garden. How his father was quite rich and had a thing about people wasting their opportunities. He and Margarita had visited out of the blue to make it a surprise visit – catching them in the pub-garden after church. Seeing them sitting there speechless, his mum almost moved to tears, his dad too which was a bit of a surprise. And all the time hardly saying a word which was a bit of a disappointment after they'd gone all that way. But on the way back it turned out they had plenty of time to themselves and it had been nice looking out of the train window at the passing countryside. And – they'd been able to squeeze in a kiss and a cuddle as nearly everyone had left the carriage to let them be alone.

I agreed it was good of the people to leave them alone like that but it was a shame his mum and dad hadn't seemed pleased to see them after all that time. But sometimes that's the way it is with parents. We shook our heads and had another drink. Thomas said he'd thought Margarita would be his father's type of woman: quiet, nice big smile, rosy cheeks, no drawing attention to herself or uttering expletives which both him and his mum hated to hear women come out with.

We both shook our heads and I said it just goes to show and he agreed with me and offered me some cheese and onion crisps.

As he'd told me about his parents it seemed fitting to say something about mine. We were similar in that I don't see much of my mum and dad which is a bit of a shame but I'm not too bothered because, as they say, these things can happen. When my wife left me I thought I'd better phone them to tell them because it's the sort of thing parents like to know about. When dad asked why she'd left I said because I hadn't satisfied her in bed and when she'd come home early from yoga she'd caught me practising on Candice. I told him it was unfortunate and not really my fault but I don't think he was listening because he put the phone down while I was speaking and he hasn't spoken to me since. I think maybe he was disgusted that my wife walked out like that and can't bring himself to talk about it. I said I'd thought about taking Candice to meet them but I wasn't sure it was a good idea. It can be awkward for parents meeting your new partner when they've been used to seeing you with your wife and they might take it out on Candice which wouldn't be fair.

Thomas agreed and shook his head and said parents were a strange bunch and I agreed and said 'I guess it's the same with a lot of people' and he nodded and offered me another crisp.

Margarita and Candice were getting on fine, chatting away like they'd known each other for years. But women do like to chat when they get together. I remember that with my wife. Sometimes she'd be on the phone for forty-five minutes to one of her friends and after when I asked her what she found to talk about for forty-five minutes she told me to mind my own business. So I did.

Two women came to stand at the bar to order drinks. They were looking at Candice and Margarita and pulling faces. They said 'are these your ladyfriends then?' We nodded and they asked after their names and we told them. They were quite nice ladies and one complimented Candice on her top and I explained that I'd bought it special because wearing my wife's clothes seemed a bit unfair. She seemed a bit surprised at what I'd said. She ordered her drink and they went back to their table to tell their friends about it.

We finished our drinks and Thomas said 'Another?' I said 'Why not?' and raised my glass to prove I meant it.

The barman came and served us. He seemed to have stopped using the f word when he was near us. Maybe he didn't need to say it any more. He asked if 'the girls' wanted their glasses replenishing. I said no because Candice likes to take her time over a drink as does Margarita.

It was while we were waiting for our beers that there was a bit of a disturbance to our right. It was the men laughing and trying to persuade their mate to come and join us.

I didn't really want him to join us because men like that should find a woman of their own instead of bothering Candice and Margarita. He was grinning and wobbling a bit. I think he'd had a bit too much to drink. His mates were watching him and nudging each other. He said 'hi' and we said 'hi' because it seemed the best thing to say and he said he'd got something for one of the girls. I couldn't see what it was at first, but then he drew his hand up and it was a stud, like one of those studs some people put in their ears and some girls put in their noses. He had tattoos on his arms. One said *England* above a naked woman wrapped in a flower that looked like a tulip. He was standing next to Margarita. Thomas had hurriedly put his beer down, just as the man said 'Hello my darling' whilst he was looking at his mates. Then he said 'I've got just the thing for you' and he took the stud and was going to press it into Margarita's shoulder.

What happened next was all a bit of a blur but Thomas had leapt from his stool and grabbed the man's arm, but the man shook it off and next thing he put the stud in Margarita's arm and there was a kind of popping sound and seconds later Margarita's head flopped forwards and both arms withered, followed by the rest of her, and she kind of folded over on her stool like one of those drunk people you see in films.

We were all watching including Candice. Thomas dashed across and pushed the man to one side. The man pushed him back and swore at him and his mates were laughing in the corner. I moved next to Candice and held her close. Thomas was stood by Margarita watching her fold right over the bar almost in slow-motion until she was finally lying there without moving.

Some people in the pub were watching too and talking in whispers and I wondered if the barman was around and if he might have something to say about it but he wasn't there at the moment. The man who'd put the stud in Margarita's arm said 'Sorry mate' but he said it in a bit of a silly voice like he didn't really mean it and he went back to his mates who were laughing and one called across 'I bet that ain't the first time she's gone down on you' and then they started laughing even more. I don't know what was so funny; it's strange the way men laugh at such things for no apparent reason. The men patted him on the shoulder and shouted 'Five pints of *Fosters* darlin'" to the barmaid who was serving round the other side.

I wondered what would happen next with Margarita flopped over the bar and Thomas stood watching her. I guessed he might have felt like smoking a cigarette but you can't smoke in pubs any more. In fact not a lot *did* happen. He just stared at her for a while like he was waiting to see if she'd stopped sinking onto the bar and then lifted her from the stool and folded her arms to tuck her under his arm. He said he was going and I said I was going too and drew Candice from her stool.

Outside the pub I told Thomas I was sorry about what had happened. He didn't say anything but just stood a moment looking up the road with Margarita's head hanging down staring at the pavement.

I expected in time he might go and get another Margarita but I didn't like to say anything about that just then. They say there are groups you can go to when you keep losing partners but it didn't seem right to be talking about joining groups or getting a new Margarita with the pair of them standing there like that with him looking pretty sad about what had happened. I could understand why he was feeling sad and knew I'd be feeling the same if it had happened to Candice, which could easily have been the case.

He hitched Margarita a little higher and said he was going and we agreed to keep in touch. He shook my hand and with

Candice right next to him, leaned to give her a little kiss on the cheek, which is what men do when they meet women or say goodbye to them. I think it was his way of saying goodbye to Margarita too with Candice and her being so similar, almost like sisters. Or having been like sisters.

We watched him head off home – Margarita tucked under his arm, her flat feet swinging back and forth in time with his steps like tiny flippers.

It was strange what had happened and seemed unfair. I told Candice she was a lucky girl; that it could easily have been her being trotted off under my arm. I think people – particularly men in pubs – should find a woman of their own instead of going up to women like Margarita and sticking studs in their arm. I won't be going to the pub again, I don't think it's the place for me and Candice.

That night me and Candice made love four times – once with her on top to help me time my thrusts. I think it was the most passionate we'd ever been together. She said the f word at least fifteen times. I think it was because of what happened in the pub and it got her thinking how lucky she was and she wanted to show it. I kissed her several times during and after, and am fairly sure she had been satisfied – as had I.

After we'd finished making love I smoked a cigarette and was thinking about Margarita – one minute sitting there chatting and minding her own business – the next...being carried out of the pub under Thomas's arm like a rolled-up mat.

Talking about these things and seeing him and Margarita striding off up the road together, her feet dangling from his arm got me thinking about whether being satisfied in bed really *does* matter. It's hard to say. Maybe it does – maybe it doesn't. And maybe it's best just not to think about it.

'You're a lucky man,' I said finally – speaking mainly to myself – and putting out my cigarette and then turning to where Candice was already in the land of dreams beside me.

* * * * *

Lady In Red

The way the woman sat at the desk in full view of the plate glass window was like she was on-show: the window was a screen, the action going on behind it like people in the movies. You could see it in the way she looked, the way she sat, the way she moved – the way she walked across the floor. The way men came over to her desk, sometimes alone, sometimes in twos and threes. The way she laughed when they laughed and when they handed stuff to her, hanging around just long enough to have her laugh a little more, hair tossed back and forth off her shoulders and then back to their desks.

Maddox had stood on the same spot ten days running: a spot across the road next to the public phone booth that no-one used any more because these days people had their own phones – cell-phones, things that never left some people's ears whatever time of day and whatever they were doing. Maddox had never owned a cell-phone. He wouldn't know how to use it and wouldn't want to use it. He had a phone in his apartment and that would do, though he rarely used that either.

What he liked about the woman was that she smiled often and was the kind of person people liked to be around. The way her hair bounced when she got up to get herself a cup of coffee or crossed the room to talk to one of the guys. And – the way she dressed. He'd noticed red seemed to be a favourite color: red top, red skirt or slacks, even one of those red ribbons tied in her hair. He liked red things too: the old subway trains, Christmas lights, the sky on Summer evenings.

So far as he'd been watching her from across the street, which was easy to do and was why he'd gone back to the same spot day after day. But now things were going to change.

Her routine was simple: a break for lunch about one-fifteen. Sometimes there'd be stuff to tend to outside of the office which meant she'd leave her desk a while and be back later. Around five-o-clock she'd start tidying up her desk and leave by the front door about fifteen minutes after that.

For close to the twentieth time in little over an hour Maddox went over what he was going to say to the woman when she left the building in about half an hour's time. He'd been watching her long enough and figured it was about time he worked out what he was actually going to say. Before that he would continue to watch her through the window.

He pulled his jacket a little tighter and smoothed his hair back though there was little need to be doing that as he had very little hair and it was more a habit, the kind of thing guys in movies did before they did something important or met someone, like a date. He'd even put a shine on his shoes before he'd left his apartment which meant it was shaping up to be a special day.

None of which stopped his heart stepping up a gear when the door opposite finally swung open and a handful of people spilled out onto the steps. One of whom was the woman, wearing red slacks and a white top, light coat slung over one arm. He knew she'd take a right. He also knew she'd walk three blocks and likely pop into a small Italian diner before continuing on her way home.

But this time it would be different. He walked quicker than usual and crossed the road before the lights. The key spot was at the end of the block at the next lights. He hoped there'd be a 'Stop' sign because it would make things easier.

There was a stop sign and smoothing the near-bald surface of his head one last time he walked up behind the woman and said…

'Excuse me miss, I'm sorry to bother you but I'm just looking for a nice little place to pop into for a coffee and wondered if there was any such place near here.'

At first it didn't appear to register which is what can happen when you spring on people from behind on the sidewalk. He saw her shrug like she wanted to make it clear she wasn't in the business of striking up conversations with guys who crept up on her in the middle of the street.

Maddox understood why she'd shrugged and didn't answer straight off which was why he'd said 'I'm sorry to bother you'.

It was then that the 'Walk' sign lit and he walked with her across the road, not too close, about two or three steps behind her, just about close enough.

'I'm only asking because I'm looking for a place for later on. And I like Italian. That's my favourite.'

They had picked up the pace together on the far side of the street which gave her time to consider her best move – whether to tell the guy to fuck-off, which, under the circumstances, she'd be justified in doing, even if it wasn't always the wisest move. There were times when you needed to tread a little more carefully; keep your distance – keeping any suspicions out of your voice and sticking to short non-committal answers – and without making eye contact. It wasn't the first time she'd been approached in such a fashion and there was usually an escape route if you showed a little patience. For all that, 'looking for a place to eat' *had* been a fairly corny line. She just needed to be on her guard. She tossed a head of hair and looked along the next block.

'There's a place further on,' she said, intent on keeping up the pace.

'Okay thanks.' He followed where she was indicating, keeping loosely in step but without getting too close. 'I appreciate it,' he said. 'If it was open now I might be tempted to pop in just for a moment to grab a coffee.'

'Well you can't miss it. Just keep walking. It'll be open.' And a few steps later added 'I'm going in there myself as it happens.' Even as she'd said it she couldn't be sure why she'd said it aside from showing a resolve not to be side-tracked by guys accosting her in the street.

'Well I don't want to be a pain miss. If I was to go in there too I'd sit somewhere else.'

'Free world,' she said. He slowed his pace just a fraction.

They continued in similar fashion. Not close enough to be making conversation or to be accused of intruding – or to hold the door open for her once they'd reached the entrance on the corner of the next block to be greeted by coffee fumes and a buzz of activity round tables most of which were already occupied.

He had watched her cross the floor tray in hand and take her place at one of the tables, knowing she knew the procedure; how you didn't need to order from the waiter if you weren't choosing from the sit-down menu.

A minute later, tray in hand, he stood behind her table, taking a few steps in each direction, looking first one way and then the other, ostensibly searching for a seating space close enough to occupy.

'Would it be okay to share a table with you just for a minute?' He stood, waiting for an answer, refusing to take it as read it was his right to sit wherever he pleased. A shrug was invitation enough given the lack of vacant seats, seeing him slide into place, easing the tray next to him on the table.

'Free world,' he said grinning. 'I like Italian.' He had settled into place and was searching for the sugar. 'Even if it's only coffee.' She watched him take three paper tubes and tear the top off each and follow its contents being emptied into the cup.

'Cake and cookies too,' he said, giving the coffee a stir. 'One a day, no more.'

She maintained her silence, resolved to keeping her distance. There was usually little to be gained from being overly hostile on these occasions. Nor at this juncture any call to be so. Which wasn't overlooking the fact he'd come out with the line about 'liking Italian'...which had seemed a bit of a coincidence. She watched him studying the surface of the coffee as he stirred and put the spoon to one side.

'This is a good place,' he said, looking round.

'There's worse,' she said.

He took another drink and viewed the painting of a bull fight on the wall opposite.

A consolation, if one were needed, was him not seeming the type to engage in conversation as such. He was too busy for such things: one minute shuffling coffee spoons then rolling bits of paper and leaving them in the trash-tray – all the more reason for keeping a cool head. Which wasn't to say she'd totally ignore him. If he chose to speak, let him speak. If needed, give him an answer – keeping it brief and where possible agreeing with whatever it was he had to say.

'Name's Maddox,' he said.

'Sadie Washington,' she spoke back, prepared to keep things on a relatively formal footing.

'That's a nice name,' he said, reaching for the first of two biscuits sitting on the saucer.

'So – you from the city?' She drank and replaced the cup.

'Queens,' she said. Maddox opened the biscuit wrapping, unravelling the cellophane strip before removing the remainder.

'Cross the river.'

She nodded and made a point of checking with her watch.

'I been to Queens,' he said. 'I like to go to the airport and watch the planes take-off. *La Guardia* and *Kennedy*. I prefer going to *La Guardia*. You know why I prefer *La Guardia*?'

She shook her head and took another drink of coffee.

'It's smaller,' he explained, taking a bite from the biscuit and looking across the table. 'I like flying,' he said. 'Though I've never ever been up in a plane...not ever.' He took another bite from the biscuit. 'Guess that sounds a pretty dumb thing to say.' Sadie was saying nothing.

'You like flying?' he asked. She took a moment before answering.

'Not really,' she said.

'Me neither,' said Maddox. 'They say if God had wanted us to fly he'd have given us wings, which is a dumb thing to say cause there ain't no God. What I like about flying...is the idea. That when you get on a plane you just sit there and next thing you're in some other big city on the other side of the world. I just like to know where all those planes are going.'

She took a drink and another glance at her watch, eager to be seen hurrying things along – make it clear he was unlikely to have her attention for too long. He turned his attention to the second biscuit.

'But I like trains better. My other name is Micky... Micky Maddox.' He took a mouthful of coffee. 'Which sounds stupid, so I stick to Maddox. You work round here?' She again took a while answering – his propensity for leaping from one line of conversation to another further reason for keeping on her guard.

'Yeh...close.'

'What do you do?'

She thought about it for a minute.

'I work for a firm designing advertising bills and slogans for businesses here in the city.' Maddox nodded.

'That sounds good,' he said. 'I guess it pays good.'

'Enough,' she said.

'Do you work alone?' She hesitated. And finally shook her head.

'There's a few of us,' she said, still far from certain why she was subjecting herself to such interrogation. 'We work as a team.'

'You got men working there too huh?' She looked up from the table.

'Who said anything about men?'

For the first time he detected an edge to her voice; a warning to back off a little?

'I'm sorry. Maybe I shouldn't be asking you these things,' he said. 'I sometimes talk about stuff that maybe I shouldn't be saying.'

'It's okay,' she said, relenting a little. Fact was...men *were* in evidence everywhere you looked in her line of work – liaising with firms and businesses – men who talked and joked and were always ready with a story. And who liked the company of women because women brightened up the place. The thing about women like Sadie was…you could have a joke with them – unlike *some* women. You could come out with lines like…

'Hi Sadie, you're lookin' good today' without anyone getting the wrong idea. She knew that, in effect, you were paying her a compliment, saying how she took pride in her appearance – unlike *some* women. And when someone added *'Sadie always looks good – any day'* …knowing he didn't mean anything by that either. What they also knew was there was a line not to cross. Which was the mistake some men made…not knowing where to draw the line.

'Yeh,' Maddox said. 'I think I know what you mean. I see guys at work too.' He had been rotating the biscuit wrapper round his finger. He moved it to one side and looked across the table.

'I pack ice-creams,' he said. 'Put them in boxes.' Sadie drank her coffee. It hadn't occurred to imagine him working, though there was no logical reason why he shouldn't be employed somewhere. He didn't appear to be nuts, just a little lonely. It was easy to forget how the biggest most bustling of cities can often be the most lonely places on earth.

'Then I write down the numbers on the list and send the list upstairs,' he said. 'I don't see much of the other people.' He'd taken the second biscuit wrapper to roll it into another tight ball and let it drop into the nearby tray.

'I'm sorry. I shouldn't be talking like this, taking up your time with this stuff about work.'

'It's okay,' she said, visibly avoiding any hint of irritation. There was something endearing in his attempts to say the right thing whilst not being too sure how to go about it.

'I like this place,' he said, looking round – back to witnessing first-hand how hectic places like this can get at this time of day.

Sadie too felt at home here – seated midst all the activity yet able to remain detached from it. One waiter in particular…

Antonio...who was always quick to catch her eye and on watching her leave knew it would only be a matter of time before she was back, often occupying the same seat – when they would exchange looks and occasionally a second cup of coffee would arrive...on the house, commonly without a word spoken.

After which there would be a train ride home. A short train ride to just beyond the river. And on leaving the train, a two mile drive to their house where her husband wouldn't be home a while because he needed to work late finalising a deal with one of the up-and-coming Wall Street firms – the latest of a number of deals that, once completed, would take their operation onto a whole new level. Which – all things considered – was a pretty amazing turnaround in little over two years.

'Two things a man needs – a good wife and a good lawyer,' he would say, making it sound like a joke during dinner when they had people round. 'The two things a man can rely on... apart from the lawyer' he would add – which was the joke.

'There aren't many other people where I work.' Maddox was back to shuffling the salt and pepper pots.

She finished wrestling with her shoulder bag, appearing to be searching for something in one of the pockets. Maybe her ticket home. Although connections were pretty frequent at this time of day. It was only a short hop over the river. She downed what remained of her coffee and prepared to leave.

'I need to make a move,' she said.

Maddox finished his coffee.

'Me too. I need to get to Penn station,' he said.

Sadie looked up.

'That's where I'm heading.' She was still fumbling in her bag, closing it and making some space on the table. She was quiet for a moment. Around them every table was full, indication it was time to be making a move.

It was as she clipped the bag and raised the strap that he summoned the courage to speak.

'You want to come and watch the trains?'

She had manoeuvred the strap onto one shoulder and looked down to check if she'd left anything on the table.

'See all the places lit up in gold letters *Toronto...Chicago... Santa Barbara...Pittsburgh.*'

She appeared to have everything but it was always wise to check.

Rising from her seat, it was difficult to avoid him completely. 'What do you say?' he said.

'I think it's time to make a move,' she repeated, checking her bag once more and looking to see if her waiter was anywhere in the vicinity to witness her departure.

Back on the street it was a similar arrangement, her leading the way – him keeping in step but content to keep his distance.

It was at the mouth of the station that Maddox caught up, looking in every direction, and then at Sadie who was about to head towards the station's entrance.

'This is it,' he said.

They made their way into the station – the heartbeat of the city – steering their way past walkways and bill-posters towards the main concourse where Sadie stopped to check with the departure board. She'd missed her connection but it was hardly an issue. She rarely had long to wait. She looked back in time to see Maddox disappear to one of the kiosks. For a moment she wondered if she'd just seen the last of him.

Until seconds later he was back, a cardboard container clutched in each hand. He handed one of the cups to her.

'For you,' he said, his eye already on the destinations illuminated several feet above them.

Sadie hesitated before drawing two knuckles of popcorn from the cup as Maddox looked up.

He stood back, his eye drifting to Sadie who was stood clutching the cardboard container a little stiffly in one hand.

'You okay? You warm enough?' She nodded but pulled the coat a little tighter.

"Cause I see you're not wearing a lot of stuff. Which makes sense. You don't want to be wearing too much stuff and getting hot.' He shook the cup. 'Because sometimes women don't always wear sensible stuff. Which is not always their fault.' He stared hard into the cup. 'It comes down to other things, like we were saying earlier.' he said.

She toyed with the beaker she'd been handed. He stopped, conscious of coming across like he had a point to make.

'There I go again,' he said. 'Back to saying stuff without thinking about what I'm saying.'

'It's okay,' she said.

He was watching her look half-heartedly at the destinations illuminated above them.

'All those places. All you do is sit on the train and next thing you know you're in the middle of one of those great cities...*Seattle...Toronto...San Francisco...Vegas.*'

Sadie had stopped looking – not least because her suppositions had been correct. None of the places Maddox was naming was indicated on this, nor – as far as Sadie knew, on any other board; at least not in this part of the terminal. The only destinations on display, a few local Long Island commuter service lines – one of which would be ready for boarding a few tracks away.

'*San Diego...Miami...Detroit...*the words continued to roll off the tongue as he watched her appear to check everything and ensure her bag was clasped shut. He turned back to the board.

'Going to make a move huh?'

With a nod she turned to go.

'That's a shame,' he said. 'It's a shame that you're leaving.'

He watched her straighten her coat.

'It's a shame,' he said. 'Like with the other lady.'

His head dipped to the pop-corn before returning to the destinations on the board – his voice directed to no-one in particular. *Vancouver...Mexico City...Hawai...*

'But it's okay,' he said.

49

Sadie had turned, Maddox watched her go, his eye following her to the far side of the concourse, his expression relaxed to a half smile.

'It's okay because there's plenty more ladies working in offices in this city. Don't you worry about that.' He was staring hard at the screen as he spoke…just like at the movies.

* * * * *

The Morning After

To a lad of nineteen years – of average looks, average build and of a generally average disposition, hitch-hiking can turn out to be a risky business. Especially the day after Stan's Twenty-first Birthday Blow-out in town, doing every pub with only the vaguest recollections of how things had transpired beyond the last two or three stop-off points. And with him – for some reason best known to everyone bar himself – winding up standing at least four rounds at the bar. The implications of which hit home first thing that morning when he'd finally got round to assessing the damage – discovering that he'd left himself with something in the region of two-pounds-fifty in his pocket, and consequently little option other than to plonk himself at what seemed a viable stretch of road just short of the motorway close to town with an arm extended and the obligatory upraised finger in the hope of not having too long to wait for a lift.

Something of a turn-up for the book then when, after some fifteen minutes of getting the thumbs down from every vehicle that went sailing past without giving him a second thought (aside from kids peering curiously through cars' rear windows) a small red sports car slowed and came to a halt a few yards ahead of him, prompting him to break into a trot lest the driver should have second thoughts and go hurtling off without him.

On drawing level he took his first glimpse inside.

The driver was a woman – maybe thirty something; he was no expert when it came to gauging the ages of older women. On confirmation she was heading his way at least for a short stretch he was given the green light to open the door and climb aboard.

It took a moment to settle, belting himself into place and turning to express a word of appreciation. Late thirties or pos-sibly early forties, she was certainly a good-looking woman, close to the 'film-star' bracket if you made a few concessions for age – accentuated by a huge pair of black sun-shades that on lesser mortals would seem pretty stupid under the grey skies of mid-April.

Allowing him time to settle she raised the shades to reveal impressive film-star looks – certainly on the mature side but in-keeping with the image typified by the vehicle she was driving. He put her in the picture about where he was heading, allowing her to reach across and check the door, watching and waiting till he was firmly in place.

'I can take you some of the way,' she said, her eye back to the road whilst reaching to slot the car into gear. 'But not all the way.' She watched him lift the shoulder bag from the floor and settle it into place on his lap.

The woman was impressive. He'd already detected an edge to the voice – the laying down of a few markers like this was *her* car and *she* was the one calling the tune as well as doing the driving. And – she was undoubtedly, what his dad would have called – 'a fine looking woman' – confirmed the moment she'd lifted the shades revealing eyes that were unquestionably film-star material: possibly more the 'woman-next-door' than the 'college cheer-leader variety' but an appealing enough prospect for an hour or so the morning after getting wrecked with Stan and the boys in town.

She didn't hang around with her driving either. Only when the speedometer had hit the three figure mark did she relent, looking leisurely to her left, pausing to ask after his name. He told her and she nodded.

'I'm Celeste Love,' she said, speaking like she was revealing the information only as a special treat. It sounded a bit corny and non-too-convincing but no less appropriate for all that as she turned in her seat to check the scene behind – presenting him with full view of a fair sized pair of boobs, not too small, not too big – just about right.

'So – where've you come from?'

Back to cruising speed she resumed her habit of following a question by looking him directly in the eye. He gave her a quick rundown of the previous evening: going into town, meeting Stan and the guys for the party pub-crawl in and around the centre. Getting a little drunk. Not too drunk. He wasn't going to tell her too much about that.

'Sounds like fun,' she said, leaning back to have the shades settle on the bridge of a shapely nose. 'Do you like parties?'

Again she had turned to face him full-on. One of these people who need to *see* a question getting answered as well as hear it – like what she was asking was a big deal that demanded her attention right down to the last syllable.

'Sometimes.'

He pulled the bag tighter on his lap and turned his attention to trying to read the signs passing at a rate of knots at the side of the road; at that moment anything linked with the consumption of alcohol pretty low on his list of priorities.

'I like *some* parties,' she said, a hand resting lightly on the steering-wheel before drifting to the dashboard where it remained a while. 'At the right time – and with the right people.' She looked across. 'I like to party, but *only* with the right people.'

She looked back, content to let the driving do the talking while she moved only to shift herself more comfortably in her seat, fingers continuing to tap away on the dashboard before returning to brush lightly against the fold of her skirt, effectively edging it to one side about three inches above the knee.

'And – I like to drive fast. Sorry if I'm driving a little *too* fast. It's just the way I am I'm afraid.'

She made a show of lifting her foot from the pedal and again turning to look him in the eye as she spoke.

'I'll slow down a little if you think I'm a little too fast,' she said. 'I'm told my driving makes people nervous. Especially younger people.' She at once broke into something close to a smile. 'I don't know why.'

Having no answer at hand nor any inclination to try coming up with one – the pair sat in silence: brief enough interlude for a hand to revisit a spot of earlier irritation a few inches above her other knee, stopping to quickly flatten the skirt back into place.

'I don't make *you* nervous do I?' Her eyes widened like it was a question that had only just occurred to her to ask. 'I'm only asking because some younger men – particularly quieter, more thoughtful men – do sometimes seem a little nervous in my company.'

She was back to the mirror, her attention drawn to a vehicle approaching hard on her rear – one of these young executive-types only too ready to show frustration at being reduced to a snail's pace by a woman driving some dippy sports car.

'Go fuck yourself,' she shouted through an open window – a toot of the horn and raised middle finger following close at hand.

'But – don't get me wrong.' She was back to the moment prior to the interruption.

'There's nothing shameful in being male *and* sensitive,' she said. 'They're qualities I find admirable in *all* men – particularly younger men.'

She lowered the window, a mane of bleached blonde hair flowing in time with the rap music bouncing from the CD player. 'It's something a lot of men – particularly younger men – often fail to realise: that women – particularly older women – are far more attracted to men of a gentle sensitive nature.'

She peered, eyeball to eyeball, lowering her glasses to check on signs of a reaction in the passenger seat. 'A description that – on first impression – would appear to fit you perfectly.'

It was on adjusting the hem-line of her skirt and relenting on the speed by easing a foot from the accelerator that she steadied the shades one last time to check all was clear in the rear-view mirror and draw the car to a halt.

'Well...this is as far as I go,' she said, turning to watch him manoeuvre himself into rising from his seat.

'Thanks for the lift,' he said, managing to raise himself sufficiently to drag himself through the door, the bag still clutched tightly to his lap.

'No problem,' she said waiting for the opportunity to switch her attention back to the road.

He stood, watching the vehicle speed off at a rate of knots, reaching over his shoulder to hook the bag into place and grimacing for would hopefully be the final stint of his journey.

'That woman got lucky,' he said, stepping his way gingerly along the grass verge. 'She came very close to getting herself banged there.'

He stopped and looked back, shaking his head at the stroke of good fortune that had come the woman's way.

'Actress or no actress – 'Celeste Love' definitely came close to getting herself well and truly banged,' he said, speaking to himself and dipping his finger into his pocket to retrieve what would hopefully be sufficient funds to cover the last few miles by bus.

* * * * *

Tommy The Pig

It was on the fringe of a small town somewhere in the depths of Sixties' northern England that a small skinny boy in short trousers emerged from a maze of cobbled streets to head in the direction of open fields punctuated by fences and a series of grassy knolls – beyond which the address listed on a piece of paper stuffed in his rear pocket was presumably to be found.

On arrival at the place, finding himself in a small yard surrounded by what appeared to be a collection of outhouses, the boy stood a moment, feeling a little out of sorts and searching for some sign of life. It was grim-looking place, the kind of place that he could do without having to hang around any longer than was necessary.

As if reading his mind a door opened and a man appeared, taking time to observe the boy before venturing down a ramp to make his way towards him. He was a stocky bullish looking man with thick set jowls and craggy features. He wore dusty overalls laden with a permanent camouflage of grey powdery film mottled in places by traces of crimson.

Avoiding eye-contact, he approached, rubbing his hands and scowling – an expedient tactic for dealing with small boys who ventured illicitly onto his premises.

'What can I do for you son?'

He spoke in a thick meaty growl that was largely lost in the upper folds of his tunic. The boy sniffed cement dust from his nose and extended a hand in the man's direction. A torn piece of paper exchanged hands and was unfolded for examination. The man finished reading the note and gestured the boy to remain at the foot of the ramp and not to try nicking anything, whilst he disappeared behind the green door.

When he reappeared he was clutching an old metal trolley – a bulky two-wheeled affair with rubber gripped handles. He stopped for a moment to catch his breath, allowing the boy to set eyes on what lay in store for him. At the lower end of the contraption was a large support cradle constructed of interwoven piping.

Perched on the piping and looking a little bemused at having been hauled from the security of his pen, was a small pig – looking a little nervous at being hoisted unexpectedly into the great outdoors. With a degree of huffing and puffing trolley and pig were nursed down the concrete slope to come to rest at the boy's feet.

The boy looked down. The pig was – truth be told – a little too large to fit comfortably on its supporting base: one end of it poking into the air, the other – its head – resting against one of the steel frames.

'Right,' the man announced, giving vent to a thick throaty growl… 'One pig!'

He dotted something on a piece of paper and handed it to the boy who withdrew a few sheaves from his back pocket and placed them in the man's hand. The receipt of money went some way to enlivening the man's spirits as he took the handles of the trolley in hand and instructed the boy to watch carefully…cos he wasn't goin' to fuckin' well go through it all again. The boy watched as the man took the handles in his meaty grip and took a few strides back and forth across the concrete.

'See – get the 'ang of it?'

The boy said nothing but followed the man's directions, taking hold of the handles in an attempt to wheel the trolley across the tarmac. It was no easy business and a source of some amusement to the trolley's owner, seeing trolley and pig weaved hither and thither as if the boy was in a state of panic or extreme intoxication.

But after a degree of tinkering with the machine's finer nuances, a kind of rhythm was established and the three of them – boy, pig and trolley – finally made it to the gate.

Having observed them thus far, the man's contribution to proceedings came to a swift halt and he turned with a chuckle to resume his cheese and pickle roll in the warmth of his office.

Out on the open road it was time to take stock, for the pair had a fair old journey ahead and the boy was keen to get going before the temperature dropped. He cast an eye on the load perched precariously on the foot of the trolley. It seemed content enough – its little belly rising and falling like a set of tiny bellows, its snout wheezing away like a big spongy valve.

On leaving the yard, first stop was the 'Gear' shop, for it was important to have the pig – whose name was Tommy – looking 'the business', and minutes later, the boy – whose name was Hector – emerged carrying a small carrier bag.

Minutes later they were set and ready to go: Tommy-The-Pig feeling, and looking, quite the ticket, decked out in a Stetson hat quaffed to one side, black plastic shades perched on his little snout and a fine egg-yolk scarf ebbing and flowing in the breeze like a feather in a wind-tunnel.

From the first tentative steps Hector kept a close eye on Tommy, checking that the straps hadn't worked themselves loose or been pulled too tight and that he was able to keep his trotters on the two plates without them sliding off and dragging along the floor. But all seemed to be in order and he appeared to be coping admirably.

Taking hold of the handles and with his now tried-and-trusted approach of arching his back and pushing the trolley at roughly chest-height, he managed to shift them some yards along the pavement. It took a deal of trial and error but a steady rhythm was finally established and they were able to put a reasonable stretch of pavement behind them before taking their first break.

Tommy – for his part – seemed to be doing fine, the scarf flailing behind him in the breeze; his posture with his thigh tops splayed open against the trolley's stanchions like a pair of fleshy maracas allowing him to take advantage of what was a whole new experience for the pair of them.

It was on reaching the summit of a small hill that the opportunity to take a break arose – chance to wipe sweat from his huge expanse of forehead and allow Tommy to cast his eye across the open landscape – the first he'd seen of the big wide world beyond the confines of his pen. But they would have to be brief; they couldn't afford to wait too long and with Tommy settled once more against the back stanchion of the trolley, they set off on their next stint along the tarmac road.

It was on the fringe of a line of houses about half an hour into their journey that they were disturbed by a strange clanking noise drifting into earshot from behind.

Seconds later, an old butcher's bike drew to a halt and a black-frocked man with a leery look about him turned in their direction. He remained on his steed for a moment, but was quickly off it, peering over Tommy like some grotesque question-mark. The man looked vaguely familiar, the kind frequently spotted floating from door to door in town, occasionally granted admittance but as often dismissed with a wave of the arm.

Leaving his vehicle hooked against the kerb, he viewed the pair through narrow squinting eyes.

'G'day sir. And a top of the morning to you both.'

Hector said nothing. He was, in truth, a little wary of strange-frocked men who appeared on the scene from nowhere full of smiles and cordial greetings.

'So what have we here?' the man continued, casting a curious eye in the direction of Tommy who had barely flinched at the man's arrival, his stare fixed rigidly on some vague point on the horizon.

'Tommy-The-Pig,' said Hector, eyeing both trolley and its occupant.

The man grunted but offered little by way of further response. He leant closer, peering earnestly into the animal's eyes.

'And where might you be heading?' he asked, his gaze drifting from Tommy's Stetson and shades to the mottled flanks of its little belly.

Hector shrugged.

'Home,' he said. The man looked up.

'Tis to the creature I speak.' He turned his attention once more to pig perched stiffly twixt the stanchions of the trolley. 'A tiny creature, yet endowed with such grace and beauty.'

Restoring himself to full height, the man was at once fumbling with the lacings on his bag, mumbling to himself in the process, his foot braced against the trolley's right wheel. Moments later, peering in Tommy's direction, he raised the bag skyward and his voice likewise.

'Sir – I have a little something here. A little 'offing' shall we say. A fragrance – of such Episcopalian power as – for one moment of your time – and the cost of a few pence – will bring sustenance of soul, and the gift of eternal-life to the pilgrimage upon which you are, by a gnat's whisker, embarked.'

Hector was puzzled. He didn't really understand the man's words and was a little put out to see his foot placed so firmly against the trolley's wheel. He was eager to be on his way and had little desire to be waylaid by strange-looking men who gazed skywards and talked gobbledy-gook. But, he was equally aware that, with his lack of stature and Tommy defenceless strapped to the brace of the trolley, they would be no match for the man and his strange mutterings. And being already wise to the world in these things, he reached to his pocket for the few pence that might, at least, get the man out of their face and get them back on the road.

The man, having secreted the coins about his person, was once more about his haversack.

Hector watched as he withdrew a tiny goblet – a chintzy-looking thing hanging from a silver chain. Lowering the goblet to within sniffing distance of Tommy's snout he proceeded to swing the thing to and fro like the pendulum of an old-fashioned clock, releasing a winsome lavender-type mist that hung

momentarily in the air before being swept away by the afternoon breeze. He tried again, swinging the chain a little more
vigorously but, again, to no avail – the vapours immediately
seized by the surrounding air and duly dispatched to some
point in the upper echelons.

The man shrugged, and giving the contraption's working
parts a quick shufti, popped it back in his haversack to be
replaced by a far more fearsome-looking gadget: a huge
cylindrical affair with a funnel at one end and a metal plunger
at the other. With half an eye on his watch and the other on
Tommy, he gave the contraption a resounding shake, lowering
the orifice to within touching distance of Tommy's snout.

'Sir – you will be familiar with the more...'wash not only
thy face, but thy ineptitude.'

At which the man uttered yet more inaudible words and
applied full weight to the plunger, releasing a noxious bouquet
of fog that, within seconds, had both Tommy and the
surrounding air gagging in protest.

'Ha – most singular!' It was on administering a second dose
that the man stood back, seeing Tommy waver and almost
keel over in his trolley.

'Excellent!' he said, straightening himself and returning his
contraption to its home in the depths of his haversack.

With a brush of his hands and doff of his cap he was once
more upon his trusty steed, sweeping the cloak abreast the
bars.

'Sir – it has been my privilege to engage, and serve you and
I thank you for your time and trouble. You may have gathered
that wherever I may travel, my trusty haversack...' He
indicated the bulky load strapped firmly between his
shoulders... 'travels with me...for he who pays the piper calls
the tune! Be assured sir, you are now – even at such a tender
stage of your voyage – endowed with such Episcopalian power
that will make your venture something beyond the all-too-
familiar stroll-in-the-park....Here is my card. G'day to you sir.
And to you too my friend...'

With which, and as if hoiked by some mystical force from afar, he was off and – minutes later – a mere silhouette dotted against the sky.

Whatever the man's line of business, his calling-card was, for sure, a most singular affair, leaving poor Tommy, belted into his trolley, coughing and heaving in an attempt to evade the man's rancid claws.

Hector, who had at least been able to make a dive for the gutter to evade the worst of the noxious emissions, was quickly back to his feet – all four feet three of him. Reaching up he did a quick check on Tommy, who, though strapped firmly in his trolley was now slumped against the stanchion wearing a glazed, vaguely psychedelic look, the scarf – little more than a dull yellow streak hanging limply from his shoulder

Grabbing the handles he turned his attention to the next stretch of road that would hopefully get them back on their way without further interruption, for they had some distance to cover and there was little to be gained from hanging around.

Thankfully, at this point the road was mostly flat and took them past a few miles of tiny black-bricked homes joined at the hip like long lines of soot, the only interruption to their vision – tiny moon-like faces peering through thick panels of opaque glass. One or two waved and Hector felt honour-bound to return the waves though he was wary of losing his grip and having the pair of them careering in the gutter.

It was as they were passing the last end-of-terrace that Hector observed what appeared to be a number of their occupants: a small battalion approaching over the brow of the hill, spear-headed by a squat buxom woman with rolling-pin arms and Popeye-features and flanked by a scrawny individual wearing a vacant look. A man very much in the shadow of the woman at the helm.

One by one the crew gained their ground, following their leader, who – having spotted Hector and Tommy approach over the brow of the hill, rolled her sleeves revealing brawny arms and expanses of thick bruising flesh.

'What's all this then?' she asked, closing in on the pair, her arms folded across her ample midriff.

Hector looked down to where Tommy lay listless and pale and still wheezing after his ordeal with the cloaked figure and his fearsome plunger.

'Tommy-The-Pig,' he said, turning his eye on the stretch of road extending some way beyond the horizon.

'Hmm...' There were mutterings amongst the ranks.

'Pickles – come and take a look at this.'

She beckoned a porky arm at Pickles – a gawky exclamation-mark of a man who drew alongside, allowing others to slot into place alongside him – all tutting and muttering under their breath.

'What's all this?'

'It won't do.'

'It's as good as naked.'

''Cept for a hat...'

'And a scarf.'

'A daft scarf...'

'Daft hat...'

'Where's your mother?' Hector shrugged, staring vainly in the direction they'd hopefully be heading before too long.

The woman flexed her biceps and stepped forwards.

'Right...Let's get to it. We'll soon have him looking decent.'

A click of fingers brought a frenzy of activity: pantaloons, jackets, miniscule hosiery – all tossed onto the scene from a portmanteau midst much ranting and a series of near-blows.

It was after much jiggery-pokery and pulling and shoving that Tommy's straps were whipped away and he found himself hoisted in the air like a chicken.

It was down to Ethel – the muscle-bound woman's elder sister to whip out a cherry-red jump suit and lilac polka-dotted top, slotting both into place, trussing him up like a freshly-parcelled haggis – the belts and buckles effectively reducing his movements to a few wheezing cries.

'Now – that's more like it,' said their leader, nodding her signal for Tommy to be flopped into place, capped, bound and gagged on the trolley.

'Now he's decent,' said one.

'Now he's proper,' said another.'

'Let that be a lesson,' said a third, joining the fray to examine Tommy more closely – particularly his rear trotter protruding from the trolley's stanchion at a most peculiar angle.

It was a job well done, but there was little call to be standing around admiring their handiwork.

Lifting the case from the floor and dumping it into Eccles' lap, their leader strode off, whistling and clicking her fingers for the crew to follow.

In little more than a few minutes the whole battalion had shrunk to a cluster of tiny ants, eventually disappearing over the brow of the next hill.

Hector watched their departure, immediately turning his attention to Tommy wheezing and puffing, trussed and gagged on the trolley beneath him. His eyes were closed and there was little sign of any movement – just a few faint flutters under the needle-hairs of his chest.

He knelt to examine the garments, toying with the idea of maybe removing them, but was greeted with such flexing of the creature's better half that he quickly abandoned the idea – the belts and buckles having been secured with such force it would be no simple matter releasing them.

Back to the trolley. Hector took the handles and leant once more into the task of pushing them beyond the line of houses to a stretch of rough unkempt ground comprised of grassy knolls and thick clumps of bushes.

It was some time later that they had left the town and its peculiar inhabitants behind, surrounded at this point by a few grassy humps, clumps of trees and the calls of wild fowl from the bushes and reeds alongside the road.

Hector had been keeping an eye on Tommy, hopeful that a change of air and a change of scenery might at least see some sign of recovery – the effects of such encounters on one so young and frail almost certain to take its toll. And – as Hector observed with another quick glance at his watch – there was still some way to go yet.

It was soon Hector's turn to show signs of weariness as he continued to wheel the pair of them past empty fields and tiny streams. Tough going, yet – devoid of the torments that had plagued the opening stage of their journey – it had its moments: not least, a chance to take in the wide open spaces with their huge towering trees and birds gliding effortlessly across the heavens, whilst beneath them, slumped across the base of the trolley, Tommy had sunk to a mood of quiet reflection, amusing himself counting the fence-posts along what was certainly the quietest stretch of road they'd encountered since leaving the yard.

It was about a quarter of a mile later following a sharp bend in the road that signs of movement on the trolley caught Hector's eye – a kind of scrabbling noise accompanied by a series of short grunts, prompting Hector to draw the trolley to a halt and look down, expecting to see Tommy maybe toying with the straps or attempting to manoeuvre himself to a more agreeable posture.

But what he actually saw was something far more amazing and, at first glance, far more startling.

Far from wriggling to a more agreeable posture, Tommy was pretty much back to his former self: perched on the trolley, wrestling first with the belts still strapped round his waist and then with the plastic bag that Hector had dumped Tommy's gear in following their encounter on the brow of the hill.

Hector could only stand and watch in amazement as – with a final fling of his trotters – the straps were flung aside and Tommy, still chomping and muttering away to himself, was back to pole-position – the Stetson, shades and egg-yolk scarf all set and raring to go.

Another turn up for the book – not least that there was more to young pigs than first meets the eye. Above all...

knowing the need to show a little patience; that the best way to deal with unwanted, and unwarranted intrusions – be they weird men talking gobbledygook or muscle-bound women flanked by numbskulls – was to simply play-the-game: lie low, bide your time, even, as and when required, 'play dead'. Then – at some later date, having found yourself a bit of solitude and a bit of breathing space – get up, dust yourself down and pick up the reins from there.

It was evidently a cunning little pig that Hector had been wheeling around for the last few hours. But – both knew they had some way to go yet and with the clouds thickening ahead there seemed little to be gained from hanging around.

It was about half a mile further that they came to a fork in the road.

Hector drew them to yet another halt, allowing them time to survey the scene and consider their options.

In one direction – pretty much the same as before: row upon row of tiny homes cluttered along narrow claustrophobic streets.

Whilst in the other direction – nothing! Just a few fields, a few trees, a few birds soaring and diving against a backdrop of ever-darkening clouds.

The pair exchanged looks. It was the easiest decision they'd had to make all day.

Not for the first time Hector reached for the trolley's handles, heading the three of them (Hector, pig and trolley) towards the wide open spaces and tiny clumps of trees.

For the moment, quite *where*, or even *what* 'home' was – seemed neither here nor there. All they knew was that it was some way off, and for now that was all either of them wanted or needed to know...particularly Tommy – sitting there, looking, and feeling, quite the ticket, decked out in a Stetson hat, black plastic shades and a fine egg-yolk scarf ebbing and flowing in the breeze like a feather in a wind-tunnel!

* * * * *

Rhino Trouble

Telephones ringing was an inconvenience Meadowcroft Wilson could do without. He wasn't keen on telephones – and far from impressed to have them ringing in the midst of his post-lunch siesta.

Dragging himself to his feet before the ringing ceased, he reassured himself it would likely be something and nothing – some traffic problem at a river-crossing or a case of shoplifting at one of the local bazaars: a mood far from quashed on hearing the cause of the interruption was nothing quite so routine, but was to do with the arrival in a local village of one of the most celebrated and ferocious creatures to stalk the land: the infamous Long-Horned Rhinoceros.

An unfortunate development on a two counts: *one* in that dealing with such creatures would be unfamiliar territory for Wilson. As a newcomer to the force he'd been assigned one of the more rural outposts where wild beasts were a common enough sight; but crime – as in *real* crime ie. killing people, stealing from them, or worse still…stealing their property, was less common than in more populated areas. And *two*…that with all remaining members of the force engaged on crowd control at a neighbouring village's Mid-Summer celebrations, responsibility for dealing with the issue was set to rest solely on his still somewhat inexperienced shoulders.

Unfortunate from the creature's point of view too, in that its reputation as one of the most feared creatures to stalk the land was by and large undeserved – a consequence of being saddled with one of nature's less flattering touches…a two foot horn stuck slap-bang in the centre of its forehead and curved slightly at its apex.

Unbeknown to most and largely overlooked by others – was that the creature also happened to be one of the noblest, most intelligent and majestic beasts to inhabit the land. And that being largely a solitary creature, it was more given to grazing amongst its own kind than cavorting in pursuit of lesser mortals. And – it was nowhere near as stupid as it looked.

Attempting to view the situation as calmly and objectively as befits a recruit attempting to make his mark on the scene, Wilson replaced the phone, polished off a large g & t and took himself into the neighbouring room where, steeling himself for the ordeal ahead, he began thumbing his way along the rack in pursuit of a suitable weapon – should the worst come to the worst.

Having little – which is to say 'no' – experience of handling any of the options available in what might be termed the 'heat of battle', it took a while deciding which might be best suited to the task. A decent sized Winchester with a lengthy barrel and the finest cross-hair sights seeming as good a bet as any. He released it from its catch and tossed it from hand to hand to familiarise himself with the feel of handling a weapon for the first time in several months.

First thing to strike him was the sheer weight of the thing. Aside from hoiking one over his shoulder in military-style parades he'd had little experience of handling a weapon in anything close to a combat situation and the prospect of carrying one with a view to actually employing it in battle was a daunting one.

In the village, the mood had subdued a little. Viewed at such close quarters, the creature seemed placid enough – rather more comical-looking than appearing to pose any immediate threat. But few were fooled. Though it hadn't, as yet, 'killed' (as in...wiped out any members of the local population) all knew it was likely a matter of time before one of them found himself skewered on the grotesque protrusion currently foraging its way through the undergrowth.

On arrival at the scene Wilson had deliberately parked some distance away, aware of the need to tread warily, assess the situation, and keep his nerves fully in check – equally aware that even a hint of anxiety would be perceived as a sign of weakness amongst the locals.

Neither hurrying nor wishing to be perceived as dawdling, he strode casually toward the creature still apparently content to bide its time foraging amongst what remaining lines of vegetation it could find – its every move coming under close surveillance from a crowd already four deep at the trackside, whilst others peered from windows or gathered on rooftops in order to secure a better vantage point. For such events were not to be missed: the age-old gladiatorial combat of *man* versus *beast*...about to be performed in their own backyard and in the true tradition of such encounters – with room for only one winner – in this case secured by means of a few quick rounds from a police-officer's rifle.

At what appeared to be a strategic spot Wilson took time out to recall advice regarding the dispatching of his weapon should the need arise: an imaginary line drawn across the beast's features as opposed to simply taking aim and releasing a few pot-shots in the region of its head or worse still – its flank, however inviting a target it might present. And that the 'kick' following the discharge wasn't immediately evident. That on striking the creature – the bullet, or more likely 'bullets' – depending on the creature's size and mood, might not fell it immediately as appear to paralyse it, after which it would, in all probability, sink to the ground with a view to taking whatever time was required – likely something in the region of ten to fifteen minutes – for its demise to reach completion.

All of which was fine in theory. But on viewing the situation first hand, taking in the creature's slothful, almost benign pawing at the ground with only a passing glance at the surrounding faces – such measures seemed heavy-handed, not to say grotesque. What was required here was surely a little cajoling – to have the creature withdraw from the scene without fuss and without drawing unwarranted attention – to put a bit of distance between them and have the crowd return to their homes secure in the knowledge that their livelihoods were once again in safe hands – courtesy of the forces of law and order (with particular emphasis on the latter.)

At thirty yards the creature took a few steps and looked up, eyeing not only Wilson but also the huge bank of spectators now jostling for position along every nook and cranny lining the main thoroughfare and beyond.

Wilson followed suit, taking a few more steps in the beast's direction before contemplating his next move.

The trick – he guessed – was to have the creature acknowledge the fact that its presence was no longer appreciated; that its backing-off would – if successfully negotiated – be to everyone's advantage without the need to resort to more drastic measures.

But already there was restlessness amongst a crowd. Why all the dilly and dallying when the beast – evidently aware of its role in on these occasions – had conveniently and obligingly presented itself for the taking – a few swiftly dispatched bullets set to settle the score once and for all?

A mood Wilson was quick to pick up on – himself aware that something needed to give, but still far from sure how best go about it.

If the worst came to the worst – with the creature facing him head-on, as at present, there'd be little opportunity to draw any line across any of its features. As things stood, the best he could hope for would be to take a pot-shot in the general region of its eyes and risk the bullet ricocheting off its tusk and go gallivanting off into the crowd.

What was required was a little manoeuvring. If he could get the creature to take a few sideways steps, adopting a less confrontational pose maybe it'd get the message: that a slow retreat from the scene without fuss and without appearing to pose any immediate threat would see it able to make an expedient though not *overly* hasty exit into the trees and off into the undergrowth.

Surprising himself at his ability to keep such a practical head on his shoulders under such circumstances – and with the gun held aloft to be clearly visible at all times – Wilson launched into a series of short, staccato steps – turning through something like ninety degrees until he was stood more or less at right angles to the creature.

Able to view proceedings from a comparatively safe distance and follow Wilson's every move, the rhino – at first curious – appeared to get the message: that the name of the game here was a touch of the old *coup d' theatre* – a little entertainment for the troops whilst paving the way for everyone – itself included – to retire from the scene with all their 'bits' and dignity intact.

Which – from where the creature was standing – would seem to make sense to just about everyone.

In light of which it immediately set about mirroring Wilson's movements – easing its way through its own series of short, if rather cumbersome steps, adopting a similar side-on pose, its eye fixed first on the audience and then on Wilson for a cue as to how events might pan-out from there – a few more steps effectively removing them from centre-stage permitting a dignified if not *too* dramatic exit over by a line of trees.

So far so good. Another quick half dozen steps saw the creature immediately pick up on the act, its head levelled in Wilson's direction to bear witness as to what might follow.

It was as it was at the point of mimicking Wilson's next move – a third sequence of steps designed to steer him towards the periphery of proceedings that a bullet ripped through the air, catching everyone – beast and Wilson included – entirely off-guard.

Glancing quickly over his shoulder, Wilson looked back in time to see the beast keel over, two of its feet wavering in the air before joining the remainder of its torso in a state of temporary paralysis – its eyes at first widening and then finally closing – to a chorus of hushed whispers followed by a smattering of applause on all sides.

Looking again to his rear, Wilson spotted a figure he recognised as one of the local sub-divisional officers, emerging from the undergrowth, his weapon hooked over one arm.

'Got the blighter…You okay?'

Wilson nodded.

The figure drew alongside, his eyes glued to the beast now lying on the ground breathing heavily with thin trickles of blood running from each nostril.

'We got wind via the radio that you had a bit of an issue with the old Long-Horned-Rhino and decided we could cope a man down. Shrewd move getting him to the old side-on elevation like that – no easy task from where you were standing… Good work!'

The officer looked at the ground, his right boot nudging the stricken heap wobbling a little from side to side.

He peered closer.

'Ugly-looking sod,' he said and then looked up. 'You sure you're okay?'

Wilson nodded and turned to go. By the time he'd arrived back at his vehicle and started up the engine the walkways and rooftops were all but deserted.

* * * * *

Baby...Baby

To Frau Hechtenstein – a ex-student from Hannover with a degree in 'Logistics' – a six month residency as house-maid and general dogsbody in the country residence of the Browns of Oxfordshire England was an opportunity not to be missed: a chance to see a bit of the world, earn a little pin-money and, above all else, brush-up on her English which – by her own admission was more a product of musty old grammar books than opportunities to engage in real-life conversations on the street – or in English country houses.

On arrival and having shown herself to be to be an eager and willing worker – and as practical and logical-minded as befits any young employee from abroad aiming to make her mark on the English domestic scene, she had been quick to settle into her new routine: taking every opportunity to observe life above and below stairs and take-on-board some of the quaint customs and mannerisms to be encountered on these shores – not least the odd sayings and fondness for light-hearted banter with its eye for innuendo and unceasing demand to be amusing; though as she quickly learnt, the trick wasn't so much to be 'amusing' as 'not serious' which – she also quickly learned – was very much the English way!

But, as a guest it was hardly her place to be commenting on the ways of her hosts. Her aim, as she'd be the first to concede, was to do her job, to do it well and hopefully gain something from the experience.

Which, in the case of the arrival of two mothers and friends of the family...a Mrs. J. Thomas of Dymchurch and Ethel Carnegie of Woodham Ferrers and their recently born male offspring was – as they say – as good a place to start as any.

Rumour was it was to be an overnight stay: chance to catch up on a bit of gossip and award their hosts opportunity to inspect the two recently arrived bairns in person having only received word of their arrival by virtue of a few hurried telegram messages a few weeks prior...

The first thing to strike all members of the staff below-stairs – aside from the inane fussing of the two mothers – was the uncanny resemblance between their offspring; not surprising, one might remark, given their most telling features hadn't yet had time to settle, but in the case of these two it really was something to behold: same shape, same height, same width, same eyes, same nose, same mouth, same podgy cheeks, same butchers-sausage arms and near identical wisps of spidery blond hair; almost as if a single individual was being presented for their inspection in two quite separate bodies; and equally remarkably – unlike the case of identical twins – without even being related. And, as if to add weight to the confusion, both dressed in identical sky-blue jump-suits with matching hats and toggles. All of which conspired to have the arguments below stairs raging well into the early hours.

'I tell you they *are* absolutely identical.'

'And I tell you they're not. The very idea is quite preposterous. No two human beings, even fresh-born babies, can be *absolutely* identical – ask any nanny or midwife – or anyone with half a brain.'

'Well I say they are absolutely identical.' Ethel the Chief house-maid whose task had been to wheel the pair round the gardens to try and get them 'off' for a while before tea, confirming that the similarities extended down-below having had a quick peek at their 'bits and bobs' whilst parked behind a bush in a secluded part of the garden.

'And I say they are too.' This time Tommy, the stable-lad. Though whether a lad raised in a world of leather and horse-whips was in a position to pass comment on such things as new-born babies was debatable.

Opinions appeared to be split pretty much fifty-fifty. But – as Frau Hechtenstein would observe from an increasingly distanced and disenchanted eye...Who cares? There would clearly be no logical conclusion to the debate. It was, it seemed, just another example of trifling pursuits designed to occupy equally trifling minds.

Which might easily have been the end of the matter were it not Frau Hechtenstein's fortune – or misfortune – to be assigned the task of supervising the two infants for the first hour of the morning following their arrival, when the mothers would be breakfasting in the morning-room followed by a tour of the family's art collection which, housed for safe-keeping in the attic, was quite inaccessible by pram or cot.

Though far from an enticing prospect, it would at least offer a temporary change of surroundings and ample opportunity to examine the two bairns at length to see if all the hullabaloo still raging below stairs did indeed carry some grain of substance.

As it turned out, a responsibility not to be taken lightly. For if the antics of the two mothers were anything to go by there was clearly more to the business of child-rearing than had ever been made clear in the minds of nurses or in manuals on the subject back home.

A case in point being the tactics adopted by the two mothers in what could only be assumed was some vague attempt to 'keep the kids amused' – which in reality seemed more a question of keeping the two mothers in a state of constant 'bemusement': a bizarre procedure involving extending the infants to arms' length before repeatedly hauling them back and forth to the tune of such lines as...*Who's mummy's little boy then...yes...yes?* And *One...two...three... and then...Baby's in the air again* as the pair were once again launched skywards before being returned to base for another round of *Who's mummy's little boy then, yes...yes?*

It was all very strange. But perhaps not entirely unexpected. For Frau Hechtenstein's advanced warning that cases of eccentricity on these shores ventured well beyond mere oddities of language had already gained some ground. Not least in respect of their cooking. For generations it appeared even the humble green vegetable had been subjected to quite fearsome treatment in the hands of the British housewife. If a simple shoot protruding from the ground was to be treated with such disdain, what chance for its nation's offspring?

But – all part of her education no doubt. And, as is the case of many a traveller to foreign shores, there's often more to observe than one really has time to take in.

That said – it was no easy task taking up her position the following morning, obliged to witness the mothers' tiresome antics – delivered, it seemed, without a passing thought for the dignity of the two bairns being hoiked to and fro like sacks of cement on a building site.

It was on the fifth or maybe sixth rendition of *One two three and then…baby's in the air again* that Frau Hechtenstein was struck with an idea she'd been toying with since her arrival and one that would, in all likelihood, settle the issue once and for all!

It was following the mothers' departure midst a further round of cooing and kisses blown across upturned palms – that she allowed a minute or two before slipping from her seat to turn her attentions to the first cot – reaching to lift the blue-suited infant, placing him temporarily on a chair, to turn to his near-identical neighbour – lifting him and placing him in the first cot, brushing him down and settling his head on the pillow. And then placing his companion in the other cot.

Standing to view the scene from above, it was quite something to behold – near enough identical to the scene she had been viewing not thirty seconds earlier!

All that remained was to wait. On their return the mothers would without question make a beeline for the two cots. At which point their reactions would be noted and the solution to the household's conundrum brought to a much-warranted conclusion.

It was some twenty minutes later that the door was flung open and, as expected, the two mothers burst in, arms outstretched to cross the floor to their cots, grasping each other's offspring and hoisting him aloft to cries of... *Where's mummy been? Did mummy leave baby all alone? Poor baby...naughty mummy... One two three and then – baby's in the air again!* To be returned to base with a quick brush-down before being laid to rest safe and sound in its neighbour's cot – without a suggestion of a quizzical look...in each other's – or any other direction.

Frau Hechtenstein watched both intrigued and to no less an extent relieved: *one* in that her duties in the two women's presence would thankfully soon be at an end; and *two* a moment to reflect that it was she – a humble foreign visitor to these shores – who appeared to have single-handedly brought the issue still raging below stairs to a head.

All that remained was to put the staff in the picture; confirming that whilst fifty per-cent of them had been correct in their supposition, the other fifty per-cent had been entirely wrong – the wee bairns were, to all intents and purposes, absolutely identical.

After which it would be back to the morning-room to put the mothers in the picture as to her little experiment and see the two offspring returned to their rightful owners. Certainly, it seemed prudent to award the pair a little breathing space. Any attempt to wrestle a child from the grasp of one doting mother in order to plonk it in the arms of another would likely be a recipe for disaster.

It was on completing her chores in the visitors' rooms that Frau Hechtenstein dusted herself down to return to below stairs to announce the results of her experiment.

Where – an even greater surprise awaited!

Everyone – cooks, housemaids, even Tom the stable-lad – were gathered at the window staring and waving at whatever had caught their attention outside.

In an instant Frau Hechtenstein was with them, nudging her way to the glass – just in time to spot the two perambulators being wheeled down the path to where a black cab waited to whisk them and their mothers off up the road to catch the next train to town!

A development Frau Hechtenstein had hardly bargained for. Here were the two distinguished guests about to make their departure without even having been presented with the results of her experiment. And with the opportunity to put the pair in the picture diminishing by the second.

She needed to think – and quickly! But at such a point as they appeared to have reached – what could she do? It was unfortunate to have the pair depart without being presented with the facts, but she could hardly be blamed for that.

And on standing back with the others to view the situation from an entirely logical and practical perspective – at the end of the day – everyone was happy....

The staff had had their bit of fun, Frau Hechtenstein had gained a few brownie-points for her morning's work, and the two mothers had set off for home wheeling the two bairns with such contentment as if wheeling their very own! If ever there was an occasion for...*letting sleeping dogs lie* clearly this was it!

And – if the eccentricities she'd encountered in this land thus far were anything to go by – no one would believe a word she said on the matter in any case!

* * * * *

Sea-Front Scenario

It was on a warmer than average April afternoon that a man in his late forties striding along a quiet stretch of promenade looking for somewhere to park himself to eat his lunch – came across one of those shelters they provide for people seeking to take the weight off their feet and spend a moment watching the world go by. It seemed as good a spot as any, chance to take in the promenade and the stretch of pebbled beach reaching as far as the promontory a few hundred yards away.

Parking himself on the end of the bench so as not to be assumed to be seeking ownership of the place he stretched his legs and breathing the warm slightly salty air, turned to his knapsack to take out a Tupperware box containing his packed lunch of a scotch-egg, bap, tangerine and a Kit-Kat.

It was as he was removing the lid from the Tupperware box that a figure strode into view, stopping a moment to eye the flat expanse of sea, turning first one way then the other, and on spotting the shelter behind – taking it as an opportunity to rest up a while and roll a cigarette.

Taking his place at the far end of the bench he took a pouch of tobacco from his pocket and a packet of papers. He appeared to be in his fifties, a thin sombre-looking chap with greying hair swept back above hunched shoulders.

'All right?' The rolling process completed he looked to acknowledge the shelter's fellow occupant with a nod whilst taking a lighter from his pocket.

For a while the pair sat in silence, neither wishing to be seen intruding on the other's privacy, until – cigarette underway –

the second man leant back to take in a little more of the afternoon air.

'Nice spot this.' He cast his eye in all directions, eventually settling on a spot close to a line of beach-huts. 'It's going back a while but there was a time when I used to bring the kids along this little stretch for a kick-around.' He straightened his legs, a nod indicating an area of tarmac stretching as far as the promenade rail. 'There used to be an ice-cream wagon parked just there, right in front of that hut. Told the kids they'd get an ice-cream as long as they were on best behaviour, and let me score at least two goals!'

He leant further into the seat, the recollection evidently a source of some satisfaction.

'Mind you that *is* going back a while.' 'Must have been about twenty years ago now.' He shook his head.

'Not that they were badly behaved kids, far from it. One's in his thirties now, married – lives with his wife in Seaford. They've got two kids: boy aged eight, girl who's six. Good kids. We see them about once a fortnight. I say 'we' – me and my wife split up about four years ago. I've been living with my 'partner' about two years now. Don't know 'bout you but I can't get used to the word 'partner'. But she's good with the kids. She's got three kids by a previous marriage, one of them up in Scotland, the others living abroad. One's got a business in Spain. He's doing all right; got two kids, another on the way. The one in Scotland works for a brewery! Good work if you can get it.'

He let the observation pass, confirmation of how these things can catch up on you without you even thinking about it – watching as the first fellow took a tangerine and set about the task of removing its peel in a single strand, its completion an invitation to sit back and have his thoughts drift to matters farther afield.

'If I had my time again I'd be working abroad.' He stopped to consider the observation. 'Better opportunities, better environment to bring your kids up.' He looked to where what remained of the tangerine was duly dispatched followed by a brisk rubbing of hands.

'Came close to it once – job in Malaga. Mate of mine had a plumbing business back in the days when they were desperate for work. Offered to make me an equal partner but it wouldn't have paid as much as I was getting doing roofing work back home so I turned it down.' He stopped to reflect on what had, at the time, seemed a wise decision – and arguably had turned out to be so; notwithstanding the fact that *real* opportunities lay even further afield.

'Australia's the place! If I had my time again I'd be on the next plane to Australia –sun...sea...the outdoor life. Chance to make something of yourself.'

He sat back, resigned to a role of spokesman for a whole generation who'd missed the boat when to making the most of their opportunities.

'Thing about Australia is – the opportunity's there if you're prepared to go out and grab it. My sister's kids moved there six years ago, place near Melbourne; best thing they ever did. He manages a sports centre – deep-sea diving, shark-fishing. His wife helps out in the office, plus she's got her own business organising outdoor parties, barbecues, that sort of stuff. They've got two boys, one's three, the other's about four now. Doing very well for themselves. Wouldn't come back to England if you paid them.'

A few feet away, tuna roll and tangerine behind him, it was all eyes on the Kit-Kat: the wrapper removed and put to one side revealing a corner of silver foil, the edge of which was eased back exposing a length of chocolate coated biscuit.

'Then there's my brother – he lives in Worcester with his family. We see them every now and then. He went into decorating with a mate but sold out when the guy's marriage hit the buffers. Invested the money and got a loan to set up his own scaffolding business –making an absolute fortune.'

A crossing of legs was followed by a swift folding of arms.

'That's the business to be in – scaffolding. Particularly now you've got insurance companies kicking up a stink every which way. Either that – or property. I've got a mate who started out with two flats. Sold 'em, went into partnership, setting 'em up on short-term lets – got an agency in to avoid all the hassle. Did okay then sold out while the going was good, set up a business selling computer games to the continent – Belgium, Holland…making an absolute fortune.'

With the tangerine and Kit-Kat finally off the scene and the Tupperware box lid firmly back in place – the first man stood to brush a few crumbs and ready himself for another stint along the promenade.

The second man looked up.

'You off?'

It was on watching him make his way alongside the line of beach-huts that his attention was drawn to a young woman pushing a pram from the other direction.

Bringing the pram to a halt and checking all was well inside the cot, she moved in to occupy the vacant seat, sufficiently close to nurse the pram back and forth in an attempt to get the kid off for a while.

The man watched, stretching his legs and adopting a now familiar pose leaning against the rear of the seat.

'Takes me back,' he said, nodding at the pram. 'It's going back a while but there was a time when I used to bring my kids along this little stretch for a kick around. There used to be an ice-cream wagon parked just there, right in front of that hut. Told the kids they'd get an ice-cream as long as they were on best behaviour, and let me score at least two goals _____'

* * * * *

The Creature In The Shed

He guessed he needed to get back. The skies had begun to darken and the snares could stay a while. His father would be busy elsewhere for the next few days and his mother rarely ventured round these parts, and were she to do so would be unlikely to spot a few near-invisible wires stretched across the allotment unless actually knowing to look for them.

He stepped carefully, needing to avoid pails and the various implements placed against the wall of a building to his left: a building he'd come to call The Shed though hardly a 'shed' in the accepted sense of the word; more a kind of mini-barn. But since he'd been a kid the word 'Shed' had somehow seemed to fit and he saw no need to correct himself at this stage. He hadn't the faintest idea what was in there. Setting foot inside it was strictly forbidden and he could only imagine it was some kind of storage area – old tools, bits of tractors and other machinery. One of the many 'off-limits' places that as a kid you tend to take for granted are none of your business. Chances are it was either half empty or full of stuff that had been there years and was destined to be there a good few years yet. Though he'd never come close to venturing inside it was a difficult place to avoid if you were on this side of the yard.

He stopped and as if to put temptation to its ultimate test – stepped across to take a closer look. Always a more enticing prospect under moonlight – its black silhouetted roof giving it a ghostly feel like in one of those old black and white films he was occasionally allowed to watch on a Saturday night.

He hadn't planned to go further, knowing better than most that the closer you ventured into forbidden places the darker the forces waiting to greet you. Forces that – for once – would be put to one side – enabling him to step to the door and with a quick glance over his shoulder, attempt to open it. Surprisingly it wasn't locked and slid open easily and more quietly than he'd imagined it would.

He stopped and stared into what was little more than a thick black hole, tempting him to throw a little light on proceedings by opening the door wider, allowing moonlight to drift in from the yard.

He had his torch, knowing it might come in useful when checking the snares. There were no windows in The Shed. No-one would have had an inkling of what was happening unless they were to venture out of the house and catch him there, which – though easy to convince himself otherwise – he knew was unlikely.

On stepping further he flicked the switch of his torch, squinting at the sudden pool of light and taking care to avoid stumbling on a rack of huge chopping things that he thought were called scythes. On the wall were a number of hooks, most with buckets or long implements hanging from them.

Another step and then a pile of old boxes. And then he stopped.

Something – or at least he *thought* something – had shuffled in the corner. Maybe a cat or dog – or a rat. He shivered. The idea of encountering a rat didn't exactly thrill him even if, on a farm, they were rarely more than a few yards from wherever you happened to be standing. He stopped again and listened, not quite bold enough to direct the torch in its direction. It was there again – a strange shuffling noise coming from over by the two crates, a bit like a dog doing its circling routine before settling into place.

He looked across to where the noise appeared to be coming from and finally steeling himself and telling himself not to be so pathetic – pointed the torch in its direction.

Surprisingly – he didn't scream or seek the quickest means of escape. He just moved to the corner of the nearest box and stared at the area between two crates.

Something was perched in the space between them – something wheezing and then relaxing – some odd looking thing that appeared to be breathing but wasn't yet fully formed – as if yanked from its mother before it was due and dumped on the straw for safe keeping. Under the glare of the torch its movements reminded him of one of the farm's fresh-born piglets scrabbling through all the gluey stuff in search of its mother. Except it was bigger and its chest bulged out more, swelling and contracting like someone trying to inflate and deflate it from behind with a bicycle pump.

The only explanation was some stray animal having stumbled through a gap in the wall, but he couldn't for the life of him figure what it could be. It was a weird looking thing, not least in that it didn't seem to have skin or fur – just a collection of muscles and veins, all purple-looking and threatening to spill onto the floor at any moment.

What it hadn't done – or shown any inclination to do – was make any attempt to escape or dash for cover which you'd have expected any normal creature to do. Almost as if it was content to have been discovered on its own little patch and saw little need to uproot itself. Which got Jimmy thinking that having got in there one assumed it could get out again if it so wished – and if its instinct wasn't to do so, then maybe it had some other reason for sticking around.....

Which was the moment for it to utter its first high-pitched squeal, almost like a sailor's whistle but fainter.

It took time for Jimmy to pluck up the courage to respond, trying to imagine how it would react to the sound of the human voice. When it came, a simple 'hi' was all he could manage.

It led to a sniffling and shuffling and slight flapping of two web-like growths that seemed a cross between fins and flippers. And then another squeal that might, even at this stage, be an attempt to communicate – but to what end?

Jimmy leant closer.

'Jimbo,' he said, the word on the tip of his tongue without him really thinking about it. There was little reaction between the crates. Just a shuffling and shifting slightly from side to side like it was waiting for something to happen and could be at the point of running out of patience.

'Okay.' Jimmy said.

He knew he couldn't afford to hang around. Being away from the house for more than a few minutes at a stretch was a risk even at this time of day. And having met little Jimbo, or whatever it was, maybe it was time to get back.

He edged his way back to the door, keeping his movements slow and simple and making small waves of the hand in the process – finally putting sufficient distance between them to turn and make his exit back into the yard.

The following day proved to be a real effort. His mum said something about him seeming quiet, which usually meant something appeared to be wrong and maybe he should tell her what it was. He was quick to reassure her and relieved to be issued with his instructions for the day: shifting a few logs from behind the wall and piling them ready for collection, cleaning out the chicken-run and helping his mum in the larder before the renovations got underway. Most of which would go some way to keeping him occupied, though since breakfast he'd suspected the temptation to sneak across the yard and take a quick look in The Shed before nightfall would be too overwhelming to resist.

It was around two thirty he saw his opportunity: his mother busy upstairs, his father off-site for at least a couple more hours.

Glancing over his shoulder, he made his way round the side of The Shed and with a final look behind, moved quickly, opening the door to what seemed an even bigger gaping hole than the previous night. He'd grabbed his torch before coming out but would need to venture a little further before switching it on.

Passing tractor wheels and the same tools from last night and stepping round boxes of bits and pieces he made his way to the spot in front of the two crates, preparing himself in advance for the sight waiting to greet him. Leaning away from the torch's beam, he looked in the direction of the two crates.

There was nothing – just the crates and a flat pile of straw. He waved the torch, left, right, up down, staring for as long as it took to confirm that the creature, or whatever it had been, was gone, and, it seemed, was no more.

He stepped closer, checking behind the two boxes and then over in the corner and back to its spot between the crates, standing and listening for evidence of movement, a shuffle or a scrabbling from over in the corner. There was nothing, the whole episode reduced in an instant to a vague memory.

Allowing the torch to drift to the floor he turned to leave. The explanation was simple enough – it had waited till the coast was clear and it was safe enough to return to wherever it had come from, presumably through some hole in the rear of The Shed; the reason for finding its way in there in the first place…a question that seemed destined to remain unanswered.

It was as much frustration as puzzlement that brought him back into the yard, with little option than to busy himself with what remained of his afternoon tasks – helping his mother take stuff off the shelves and later finishing clearing space out back of the kitchen.

But the image of the little guy sitting there in the darkness wasn't about to go away. And would nag away at him for the remainder of the day – knowing he *had* definitely been there and he wasn't imagining it. Reminding himself that with creatures of the wild, things like night and day were different. The change from one to the other – a different proposition than to us and to do with stuff we don't fully understand. Plus, creatures like Jimbo were almost certainly creatures of habit, which meant the chance of it putting in another appearance – like tonight for instance – was not inconceivable.

A chance Jimmy would be loathe to miss out on.

With tea behind them and night virtually upon them, Jimmy seized his chance, closing the rear door quietly behind him and stepping carefully across the yard to the door of The Shed, easing it open, torch at the ready.

Stepping lightly, he made his way past the instruments and bits of machinery – past the boxes to the point he'd stopped at both previous visits. Stopping to peer into the corner, torchlight at the ready.

Even before the beam had found its target, the rustling and stirring was back, clearly audible from where Jimmy was standing. And seconds later under the full beam of light there was little Jimbo – perched once again between the two boxes, staring, sniffling. And – on spotting Jimmy and with recollections of the previous evening uppermost in his mind – raising the flippers or fins and extending them in Jimmy's direction.

Jimmy felt obliged to respond, extending his arm to a point where making contact would be possible; when it happened – warming to the sensation of Jimbo's spongy limb brushing against his hand.

It was accompanied by a curling sound, the flipper still outstretched. Only when it felt appropriate did Jimmy reclaim his hand, and then slowly like he didn't want to be seen causing offence.

'Hi,' he said…another return to the events of the previous night.

He'd been right; Jimbo *did* exist, if nothing else, proven by the act of making simple contact. That and the tiny whining sound, though understanding such sounds wasn't really the point. People talked to animals all day long without them understanding a single word. And people like his gran talked with no-one listening or understanding a single word.'

But the opportunity to communicate was there and he decided he might just as well take advantage of it: filling him in on a few details back in the house: his mum, dad and his sister Nina. 'She doesn't know I'm here either, but she's too small for it to matter.' Jimbo's head turned a fraction and seconds later emitted another high-pitched whine – somewhere between a squeak and a squawk.

'They're boxes that you put stuff in,' he explained, seeing Jimbo's eyes turning from side to side. 'I don't know what's in them either.' Jimbo shuffled on the straw, its veiny, purpley bits pulsating under the light of the torch, a bit like a pet undergoing surgery on the vet's operating table.

'Nice little corner you got here.' Jimmy too was looking round, half envious at the space Jimbo had marked out as his own. 'Good place to get away from it all.' His gaze drifted to the scythes and strange metal implements hanging from the line of hooks on the opposite wall.

Jimbo shuffled a little on his straw and did a quick excavation beneath his right flipper. He knew the likelihood of Jimbo understanding anything he was saying was nil; but knew that wasn't necessarily the point. That there are times when it's good just to have the chance to speak; to say what's on your mind.

But he still needed to keep an eye on the time, and before long found himself looking anxiously in the direction of the yard.

'I need to get back,' he said, still nervous at being spotted and resigned to having his time in The Shed limited to a few minutes at a time.

As he drew himself to his feet Jimbo raised another flipper and proceeded to forage around beneath it.

'Got to go,' Jimmy said, backing his way towards the door leaving Jimbo watching him leave until, on reaching the door, he ceased to show interest.

Later – much later – with the house in darkness and left to the comforts of his own bed there was much to speculate over – like exactly *who* or *what* was Jimbo and where he had he come from? A creature from the forest was still the most likely explanation, but in many ways it just didn't seem to fit. No creature he'd ever heard of looked remotely like Jimbo with no fur or skin to protect him and his insides all pumping away, all full of blood. And why would he come and go like he was doing, leaving the forest behind to creep into a shed at night to spend the night on a bed of straw? Quite apart from how he was getting in and out of the place.

It was with sleep finally about to engulf him that Jimmy had his explanation: the *only* explanation that fitted; that little Jimbo was not of this planet at all. That he was a visitor from some far-off planet: a creature whose home was somewhere amongst the clusters of stars whose occupants were quite likely peering back at him at that very moment through a crack in the curtains. A creature who – midpoint in his intergalactic travels – had steered his vehicle, or whatever had brought him here, through a tiny hole in the clouds where – in the midst of a dark secluded forest – he had landed in secret, and, on abandoning his vehicle and investigating further, secured temporary accommodation in the closest available building.

The more he went over it the more he liked the sound of it, and – the more convinced he was that Jimbo was, indeed, not 'one of us'. But was – in fact – a creature from Outer Space.

The day that followed also seemed to last forever until, with tea finally behind them, Jimmy crept once again across the yard and slid the door open, tip-toeing his way past the first few boxes to get some way inside without needing the aid of the torch. It still took a moment to get accustomed to its glow, stepping his way back to the spot where, even before his arrival, he was aware of a shuffling and seconds later, under the light of the torch, able to set eyes on little Jimbo slotted comfortably between the two crates...a little frustrated that no-one was around to witness what was happening here: little Jimmy, a kid on Planet Earth – the first human to make contact with a creature from Outer Space!

It took a while for Jimbo to do his usual thing of getting his straw ready for the night ahead. Once settled Jimmy reached into his pocket to take out something wrapped in blue and silver paper.

'Chocolate...' he said, raising the chocolate bar he'd smuggled out of the house to view.

Jimmy bit off a corner and breaking off another piece handed it to Jimbo. The head wavered a little, the flipper reaching

tortoise-style, no doubt wary of accepting gifts from creatures
he wasn't sure about. On investigation it quickly retracted –
the piece of chocolate firmly in his grasp.

'You're lucky,' Jimmy said, watching Jimbo's tiny mouth curl
and chomp on what was likely the first piece of confectionary
he'd consumed in his life. He broke off another piece and
extended his hand. This time Jimbo wasn't so cautious.

'Here on Earth eating chocolates is about the only thing
you get to do without being watched,' Jimmy said. 'I guess it's
different up in Space where it's not so easy to keep an eye on
what's going on. Or maybe they've got better things to do than
sit around eating chocolate.'

Jimmy stopped to break off another two pieces, offering
one to the flipper that grasped it instantly and shovelled it into
its mouth, making Jimmy do a quick count on how many of
the remaining pieces he was prepared to part with.

'Don't go making yourself sick,' Jimmy said. 'Talking about
Space___'

Jimmy broke off another piece.

'Down here things ain't half so exciting.'

He handed the piece over.

'On a number of counts.'

He broke off a final piece and held it out, seeing it whipped
immediately from his grasp.

'But mostly on account of Mr. Scratch. He knew what he
was saying would be some way over Jimbo's head but that
wasn't the point, Just because he wouldn't fully understand
it didn't mean he shouldn't get to hear about it. He'd been
forced to listen to stuff since the day he could walk – and most
of it had gone way above *his* head too.

He looked to where Jimbo blinked and cocked his head
from side to side.

'Who answers to the name of….The Devil – Mr. Scratch is
what they sometimes call him when you're little.'

Though appearing to have his attention there was no
reason to assume Jimbo was understanding a word he was

saying. But – like earlier – 'understanding' what people say isn't always a reason for saying stuff round here. Chances are in Space they didn't bother with things like Mr. Scratch and Devils because there's no-one to tell you about it, or listen – except where you come from – and therefore no need. But what Jimbo needed to understand if he was planning to stick around, was that down here things are different. That it might look all nice and cosy with houses and cars but there's stuff going on that causes all kinds of trouble.

With a sigh he stopped chewing and wrapped what remained of the chocolate in silver paper.

'Which I have to say is why I kind of envy you – drifting from one side of the universe to the other with no-one telling you what to do or trying to tell you *why* you're there or what you should be thinking while you *are* there. Know what mum and dad used to tell me when I was little – and still do from time to time?'

Jimbo looked up, his head hooking rapidly from side to side.

'That the greatest stunt Mr. Scratch – The Devil – ever pulled...was convincing the world he didn't exist!'

Jimmy was looking hard at the two slits that were Jimbo's cat-like eyes. There was a fluttering of fins – a shifting of weight onto his other side. A reminder, if one were needed, that once again time was against them and he needed to get back.

Rising from his seat he straightened his trousers, painstakingly removing any traces of straw. He looked back as he made his move.

'I gotta go,' he said. 'But remember what I said. You are one lucky guy Jimbo.'

A huffing and puffing in Jimbo's chest was followed by another quick turn on his straw.

It was an arrangement that came to suit everyone – Jimmy's parents too in so far as they were currently occupied re-designing the kitchen to what his mum referred to as an 'open-plan' look. It was strange how older people were always wanting to do stuff to their homes, constantly adding bits here and there or even bulldozing the place to the ground the minute they'd bought it. And they say kids are easily bored.

Still – it kept them out of the way, especially after tea, which meant there was less likelihood of him getting caught creeping outside. Though by now he'd stopped getting too anxious about it – their meetings as much a feature of his day as climbing out of bed in the morning and getting back in it at night.

Which – on reflection – may have been the root of the problem: taking things a little too much for granted, particularly once the door to the house was closed behind him.

It was early the following week that Jimmy's closing The Shed door and making his way beneath the scythes and bits of machinery, was followed by a voice – repeated the moment he spotted little Jimbo ready and waiting on his bed of straw.

'James!' He knew it was his mother. Footsteps followed the door closing for a second time.

'James!' The voice suddenly got louder,

Jimmy froze and instantly looked to where Jimbo was immediately up from his spot between the crates – instinctively seizing Jimmy's hand and squeezing like he'd never squeezed before – the pair hanging in there like they were never going to let each other go.

For the first time Jimmy was aware of the strength in those tiny flippers. A strength resulting in a succession of flashing lights and a jolt inside his skull that sent him spinning – the tools, the hooks, the door.... the roof suddenly so close he could almost touch them. Until in an instant...they all vanished!

It was with a further jolt that he woke – finding himself between two huge crates...his head easing from side to side above tiny flippers and blood-vessels so warm he felt they might burst onto the floor at any moment.

Whilst just a few feet away Jimbo stood in tee-shirt and trousers brushing himself down.

'James! What on earth____' Jimbo placed a placatory hand on an extended arm.

'It's okay mum. I can explain.'

Allowing herself to be led by the arm the pair made their way out into the open, Jimbo escorting her to the door through which Jimmy had entered only moments earlier.

'James, will you please_____'

'Shhh___I'll explain everything,' Jimbo said.

Her forearm firmly in his grip, they made their way across the cobbles to the rear door, where they stopped before reaching to open it.

'But first – we need to get a few things straight....'

Jimmy watched their departure through tiny eyes that were little more than pin-pricks in the roof of his head, able to do little except shuffle on his bed of straw and utter the loudest, most piercing cry he could muster – a cry no doubt destined for the farthest-flung corners of Space.

Whether anyone would be listening was another matter.

At the closing of The Shed door he turned to nestle comfortably in his space between the crates – now able to hear nothing beyond a deep and near-deafening silence.

* * * * *

Changes

Getting to the place had been a more convoluted business than he'd bargained on: gauging the bus times, allowing for the walk from the centre. But he had his map and felt vindicated in bringing it. He hadn't been sure whether to bring it or not at first.

For the third time he opened it at the bit he'd folded back and wiped sweat from his forehead. It was the right road; you could see it on the map leading off from the built-up bit but the heat made it difficult to concentrate.

Struggling to avoid the sun he replaced the map in the holdall along with the water bottle and the other bits and bobs.

Sure enough he'd only gone another quarter of a mile when he came to what appeared to be the place set back from the road, the whitewashed walls emphasising its modest appearance – somewhere between a clinic and a small roadside church.

He'd been standing for a minute just to make sure he *had* got the right place when a figure emerged from the rear – a man dressed in a black overall, a cap pushed back on the side of his head.

Davis approached the door and acknowledged the man with a nod. The man explained he was the superintendent – likely a key figure when it came to the day to day running of the place. He was an older man with a growth of whiskers and a thick-set look. He reached for a clip-board and a pen.

Davis confirmed he was the son. The man nodded and struck a tick on his sheet.

'This way.' He put his clipboard to one side and reached to his belt for a bunch of keys.

Inside was extremely dim after being out in the sun. He was led into a small room where the air felt suddenly cooler like a vestry at church.

The man stood back letting Davis enter first.

Davis looked inside the room.

It was painted white but there was cold grey feel about the place. A jug of roses on a table and a display of larger yellow flowers on the far side were an attempt to give it a more homely feel, which kind of worked but not entirely – which was probably the way they intended it to be.

Davis stepped to the middle of the room and peered into the casket. For several seconds he did nothing other than stand and stare.

The superintendent had retired to the entrance foyer with his clipboard.

'I'll leave you for a few minutes,' he said. 'If you want me I'll be in the room on the left.'

He turned to go.

Seeing her lying there, the colour of putty laced with what appeared to be the beginnings of a spider's web across her eyelids and forehead, was strange – but not as strange as he'd imagined. He thought about it for a moment and then leant a bit closer. He had an idea to take one of the chairs from the semi-circle and put it alongside her for a while so he could both sit and stand. The chair wasn't particularly comfortable but it didn't matter, that wasn't really the point.

It was strange – partly because he'd never done this sort of thing, nor really thought about it much. Strange too because lying so still with her eyes closed, you half expected something to happen, as if she might wake at any moment – and even stranger knowing that however long he was there, seated or standing, that would never happen.

Seeing her like that brought to mind what might be regarded as her 'parting shot': a line going back to when they were younger and she and his dad had spent a fair amount of time arguing. It was her way of ending the argument – storming off into the kitchen, vowing that there were 'going to be changes in this house'. Once, twice, maybe three times a week there were going to be changes. And once, twice, maybe three times each and every week – they'd fail to materialise. One thing he'd learnt as a kid living at home – that some things are destined never to change.

He suddenly realised he was hungry. Looking at his watch reminded him he hadn't eaten anything earlier as he hadn't been sure about the time. He also wanted a cigarette. He wasn't sure about smoking in the room. He'd best go outside.

The superintendent was stood outside his door. He said he liked to give people space and suggested he go outside for a cigarette. He said he'd join him as he hadn't had a cigarette for a while.

The light outside stung his eyes. It was quieter round the rear of the building but the sun seemed to weigh even more heavily. The superintendent offered him a cigarette but he said he'd rather smoke his own. Smoking cigarettes got them talking. The superintendent asked if he'd come far. He said not really. The superintendent nodded and wiped his forehead, saying he was lucky because he only lived a mile away which meant he didn't have to get up too early in the morning. Davis said he didn't like to have to get up too early in the morning because he often didn't go to bed till fairly late at night. The superintendent nodded and took another smoke on his cigarette.

It was extremely hot round the rear of the building – too hot. When he enquired about the possibility of grabbing something for lunch, the superintendent gave him directions to a café about quarter of a mile down the road. It was nothing fancy but it would do. Davis made to go. The superintendent explained he'd be around when he got back and there'd likely be others arriving soon so he'd be on-site throughout.

The café was okay. He had sausage and scrambled eggs and two cups of tea. Then he smoked a cigarette and did a check with his watch. Like the superintendent said...when he got back there'd likely be others there. He thought about it for a minute and then finished his tea. He thought about leaving a tip but decided not to.

The thing about going outside after being indoors is how much the brightness affects you. It struck him between the eyes and made him wince. And hurried him along. The last thing he wanted was to be spending any longer in the sun than was necessary.

The superintendent had been right. People had arrived in his absence. He knew as soon as he got back and the superintendent put him in the picture: that about six people had arrived, women and men. That they were in there now, just to let him know.

Davis contemplated going round the rear of the building for another cigarette but decided to leave it for a while.

When he went into the room it seemed even darker than before. Figures were seated in a semi-circle, mostly dressed in black. It wasn't easy to make them out but he recognised his Aunt Clementine and Aunty Nora, then his Uncle Stan. His Aunt Lysander and her husband whose name he couldn't say because it was a strange foreign name. There was another woman he didn't know but it seemed best not to create a disturbance by finding out who she was.

When he entered they looked up at him like they wanted to see his face. He wasn't sure about giving them a kiss. Sometimes that was what happened when he met them not having seen them for a while but that was usually at things like Christmas. And besides, they might have been crying. It would seem a bit odd to be kissing someone when they'd just been crying so maybe he wouldn't bother, unless they called him over and made him kiss them.

'Dear dear,' one said. He thought it was Aunt Clementine.

'Sad business,' said Aunt Lysander, looking up, watching him take his seat. He wasn't sure whether the comment was aimed at him.

He was asked if he was bearing up. He thought it was Aunt Clementine. He told them he was. Aunt Lysander said again it was a sad business and shook her head from side to side. He told them he'd been to a café for a bite to eat which explained why he hadn't been there when they'd arrived. No-one said anything but Uncle Stan nodded.

Aunt Lysander pursed her lips and fixed her eyes on the jar of roses.

'You never really think about it coming to this, but when it does....' There was no conclusion to the sentence and no-one said anything about what happened when it came to this, probably on account of it not being an issue. His uncle with the foreign sounding name breathed heavily and shook his head.

The door opened and three more people were admitted by the superintendent. They were dressed in black too and it was difficult to make out their features stood against the door. He wondered if he should have worn black, but he didn't have anything black so he couldn't. Wearing something black would come later.

Before taking their seats the late arrivals passed the others who remained seated. They took their turn shaking hands or in some cases planting kisses on cheeks. They took their seats to the left of the others and one who he recognised as Beryl, one of his mother's friends, leant forwards in her seat to speak to Aunty Nora and Aunt Lysander. He knew her as Beryl Aftershave because when he'd been younger and he'd been obliged to give her a peck on the cheek when they'd met, there'd been an aroma about her that reminded him of aftershave, or made him think of aftershave. Either way the name had sort of stuck. She caught his eye and gave him something not far short of a smile, but not exactly a smile. Her husband had died of a debilitating disease a while back. He didn't know any of the details.

It occurred to him that seated like that in a semi-circle was a bit like being in a small theatre; everyone in their places waiting for the curtain to rise – in this case on a casket flanked by a jug of roses and yellow flowers.

'Sad business,' Aunt Lysander said again, shaking her head. Her husband nodded. He tended to go along with whatever his wife said, particularly on occasions such as this. Which was the way it was with a lot of the older men.

Aunty Clementine turned to Aunty Nora to confirm what time it had happened; 'confirmed' because she was fairly sure of the answer but just wanted to be reminded of it. Aunty Nora told her it was just after six-o-clock. Aunty Clementine nodded and straightened herself in her seat.

Beryl asked him if he'd been there when it had happened. Davis said he hadn't and wondered if he should have said that because maybe he should have been there – being her son. But he hadn't known what was about to happen so he couldn't altogether be blamed. And saying he'd been there would have been lying; maybe a white lie but still lying, and meant he might have been asked for more details which he'd have had to make up.

'Well – she's at peace now,' Beryl said.

'Finally at rest,' someone else said. He thought it was Aunty Nora but he couldn't be sure.

Though he was glad to be out of the sun it had left a dry feeling in his mouth. Maybe it was the heat, or maybe just the occasion. He wasn't sure about taking his bottle of water from his haversack but then he couldn't see why he shouldn't. It took a while to get the lid off because it was still attached to the bottle. It tasted cold and sweet and when he'd finished he popped the cap back on.

'Finally at one with the world.' He thought it was Aunty Clementine speaking. It seemed an odd thing to say because she wasn't really 'with the world' now. But he knew it was the kind of thing people say and on these occasions people don't always mean exactly what they say.

'Her troubles finally behind her,' said Uncle Tom who had short legs that always seemed extremely far apart when he walked – or *were* extremely far apart; it isn't as if that sort of thing can change from day to day. He was pleased to be sitting down after being on his feet for so long. The sun, especially *this* sort of sun, was a bit too much for him. He was wiping his brow and nodding.

'Wrapped up in her old kit-bag,' someone said – possibly his uncle with the funny sounding name.

'Still – she didn't have a bad life,' someone else said. He thought it might have been Aunty Lysander but he wasn't sure. It sounded like a woman's voice.

'She had her ups and downs.' Uncle Tom nodded and said something to Uncle Stan who agreed.

'But not too many downs.'

It occurred to Davis they maybe thought he wasn't saying much considering they were all there – him included – sitting next to the woman who'd brought him into the world. But sometimes that's the way it is with mothers. It also occurred that he hadn't offered anyone a drink from his bottle. Then he thought maybe it wouldn't matter because it wasn't really the occasion for passing a bottle of water round and they weren't the sort you'd see drinking water from a bottle, only from a glass or a cup.

It wasn't long before he felt he needed a breath of fresh air and a cigarette. Smoking a cigarette in the room didn't seem the right thing to do so he got up and said he was just going to get a breath of air and smoke a cigarette. He didn't wait for an answer because he didn't expect there'd be one.

Outside, the sun hit him. He winced and shook a leg to bring a bit of life back to his joints and saw the superintendent's door ajar. Seconds later the superintendent appeared and joined him on the steps. He asked how it was going. Davis said it was going okay but he needed a breath of air and a cigarette. The superintendent said he'd join him in a cigarette. They took a few steps just to make sure the smoke didn't find its way indoors.

Hot,' Davis remarked, wiping his brow.

The superintendent flicked ash from his cigarette.

'Too hot,' he said. Davis agreed.

The superintendent asked if he'd found the cafe and Davis told him he'd eaten sausage and scrambled eggs. It had been okay. The superintendent said there were worse places to eat. Davis took the opportunity to ask what time they stayed open till, though it sounded odd putting it that way. He said they tended to play things by ear; that they didn't have a definite time but round six-o-clock was usually the time for locking the door. Davis looked at his watch. It was well short of six-o-clock but it wasn't likely to be an issue because he wasn't likely to be around as long as that. He told the superintendent who said it was all the same to him and he just had his job to do.

The superintendent had backed himself against the wall and hitched his foot into a more comfortable position.

'Strange business,' he said, straightening his back.

Davis nodded. There *was* something strange about it but it wasn't easy to pin-point exactly what it was. He thought maybe it was the idea of people lying there never to wake up again – though peering at them from above you half expected them to do exactly that.

The superintendent told him about his dad's mother who'd 'gone' whilst eating her Sunday lunch. 'Just sitting there, and the next minute – gone. Face down in her roast dinner.' He drew on the cigarette saying how it had happened one Easter Sunday, which is strange seeing how Easter is more to do with things beginning and growing. Davis asked it if was one of the reasons he'd become superintendent. He said 'no'. He'd just seen the job advertised and applied for it. They'd said you needed good time-keeping and a sense of organisation. He said he'd had these things stemming from when he was in the army. Which was what he'd said in the interview and was maybe one of the reasons he'd got the job...being in the army.

Davis finished his cigarette and wondered about stubbing it out on the ground. He'd wait until the superintendent dropped his on the ground and stubbed it under foot before following suit.

They made their way back. It was too hot to be outdoors any longer than was necessary. Indoors seemed almost dark, like sitting in someone's cellar. One or two looked up when he returned and watched him take his seat. Aunty Clementine blew into her handkerchief and sighed. She turned to Uncle Stan.

'I suppose we always knew it would come to this but somehow you don't expect it to.'

Uncle Stan made a clicking sound between his teeth.

'But at least she's at rest now,' Beryl said, or he thought it was Beryl; he couldn't be sure as she was furthest away from him.

'Gone to a better place.'

'Gone to join Tom.'

'They'll be happy – back together after all this time.'

Aunty Lysander's husband said something about time passing and no-one ever really noticing it passing. Aunty Nora said there were occasions when time almost seemed to come to a standstill.

'On occasions,' Aunty Clementine remarked.

'From time to time,' Beryl said.

What was interesting was that no-one had moved, as if getting out of your seat was uncalled for – like standing to straighten your trousers during the vicar's sermon.

'Sad business.' Aunt Lysander brushed a hanky across her features and turned to the woman whose identity he didn't know.

'Very sad.'

'But – she's rested now.'

'Finally at peace.'

'At one with her Maker.'

Davis took his water bottle from his haversack and unscrewed the top. He gave it a few seconds and then tipped the bottle into his mouth.

'Odd that it should come to this though.'

'Still – she looks rested.'

'Tom'd be happy to know she was looking so rested.'

Fingers tightened on the handkerchief Aunty Nora had been gripping for some time and he was asked about his immediate plans. He said he wasn't sure, he'd wait and see.

A little later he felt like a cup of tea and a slice of cake. When it got to the early hours of the afternoon he often had a cup of tea and ate a slice of cake. He gave it a few minutes and stood to let them know he was going to get a cup of tea and a slice of cake.

Returning to the sun was a double-edged sword: relief to be breathing outdoor air again but stepping right back into the sun!

On his way out he acknowledged the superintendent who was tending to something in the corridor. He explained he was off for a cup of tea and a cake but he'd be back. The superintendent nodded and turned to his room.

The heat made him step up the pace. It was the same woman serving as before. He ordered a pot of tea and a blueberry muffin. He liked blueberry muffins as long as they weren't too dry and didn't fall to bits when you were half way through it. This one was okay.

He took his time, lighting one cigarette and a few minutes later, a second which he only smoked half of. Bearing in mind what the superintendent had said he looked at his watch. He guessed he had plenty of time but thought it best not to leave it too long before he got back.

Back outside he regretted not bringing a hat which would have offered some protection from the sun. He met the superintendent sweeping up outside the door. He stopped what he was doing and called him over. Putting the broom to one side he informed him that the others had gone. He went inside and returned with a clipboard.

'It doesn't give up does it?' He was looking at the sky as he spoke.

'Left about ten minutes ago,' he said. 'So – it's all yours.'

Back in the room the light was almost non-existent after being outside. It seemed strange to be in an almost-empty room – almost, but not quite.

Standing over the casket reminded him of when he'd first got there; the jug of roses on one side and the vase of yellow flowers on the other. And, like before – for a while he did nothing but stand and stare. He contemplated taking one of the chairs from the semi-circle but decided not to.

It still seemed strange to see her lying there like that – almost on the verge of waking and saying something.

Sufficient to have him look over his shoulder and lean a little closer.

'There's going to be changes,' he said, mouthing the words close enough to be little more than a whisper – and then looking to see anything had registered.

She didn't even blink.

Which he guessed had been the point all along: that there were *going* to be changes – not that they'd actually happen.

He stepped to the door and looked back.

'See you mother,' he said, and then went outside to where the superintendent was in the process of closing the windows.

'Finished?' He was fastening the last of the catches. Davis nodded and made his way through the door.

It was on stepping into daylight that he noticed something was different. He looked up. It took a moment to realise the sun had temporarily hidden itself behind a huge white cloud.

The superintendent saw him looking up.

'Thank God for small mercies,' he said.

Davis nodded, making his way back onto the road and reaching into his knapsack for his bottle of water.

* * * * *

Hands Across The Sea

Mi Yung had fixed her second meal of the day: a gruel-like concoction knocked together with a few berries picked some way from the building, a few oats from the sack in the corner topped with a little milk, formed by mixing the white powder from one of the tubs beneath the counter. Taking her seat on the stool she spooned the gruel into a mix and fed herself with it, drawing her smock around her to help keep out the chill.

Having eaten and on fulfilling the first of her two duties of the day – giving the two canisters a shake and doing a quick check the contents – she climbed from her stool to complete the second: a meticulous wiping of the picture of Dearest Leader with a soft cloth, working from top to bottom of the frame and then from side to side to ensure that not a speck of dust could be spotted. Then taking a few paces back to make sure the picture was its exact horizontal position measured against two pencil marks left on the wall for the purpose. After which she would settle on her stool to pursue a daily reading from the volumes of books stacked on the shelf: two beautifully bound collections capturing every detail of their revered and universally adored Leader's love for their country and his people (*people...is in...*the members of his immediate family) whilst heaping applause on their perennial struggle against the oft-sung masters of imperialist aggression...The Americans – a people of whom Mi Yung knew little beyond their well-documented attempts to bring their country to its knees and their soldiers' fondness for slaughtering children as fellow-soldiers stood mocking at the roadside.

On completing her day's reading she would replace the book on the shelf to return to her canisters, giving each another stir. And the same with the powdered milk, giving it a shake and then replacing it beneath the counter where it would remain until the evening. Such was the day of Mi Yung – a day that had its beginning, middle, and end. And would follow a similar pattern...*ad infinitum*

Some hundred miles or so to the south – Steve Kember drummed idly on a car's steering wheel, partly to relieve the boredom and partly to keep in time with the CD currently playing on his portable machine powered by batteries purchased at the Tourist Shop prior to his departure. Passing through of one of the most impoverished environments on earth behind the wheel of a motorised vehicle had its moments, which – he'd have to admit – there was little shame in drawing some satisfaction from. His only real concern – at some point needing to find a spot close enough to running water – chance to grab a wash and fill his kettle for the night to come.

And to reflect on a convoluted merry-go-round of wheeling and dealing: a behind-the-scenes diplomatic wrangling that would have been unthinkable only a decade ago – culminating in the issue of a Four Day Pass allowing independent travel without restriction, twenty-four hour guides or any hint of military presence. In diplomatic circles something of a coup – though as it turned out, a gesture from the powers at be as indication as to how events were to shape up in the wake of the new millennium.

Kember's role – to take possession of the appropriate 'documentation' from a hotel desk at a few hours' notice and take charge of his registered vehicle immediately: the 'pass' permitting freedom of travel for up to four days – though exclusively off his own bat.

It was some twenty miles further that the road straightened and bordered a plateau, an expanse of fields giving a clear view of a rapidly darkening sky. Finding a suitable spot was a priority, but with plenty of fields ahead there'd likely be an opportunity before too long. If only to relieve the boredom a little more he stepped on the gas and leant more firmly into the wheel.

Mi Yung had laid out her nightly attire and was about to close the day's proceedings with a routine end of day treat – a drink of chocolate beans mixed with water and a little powdered milk. Relishing the warmth oozing through the pot she crossed the room to take up her customary late night spot at the window: chance to view the moon and its myriad of stars, always something of a spectacle at this time of year. Chance too to bring a little warmth to tired bones and – reflected in the glass – vague images of a room full of faces, one or two of which would, from time to time, break into something akin to laughter.

It was whilst drawing her imaginary patterns in the glass that a less familiar light appeared somewhere on the horizon, a light that appeared to be hovering much closer to Earth and – unless she was much mistaken – giving every indication of heading her way.

She at once stepped away from the window, placing her cup on the counter.

Kember had spotted the trees a while back. Where there were trees there was likely a stream. And where there was a stream there was a chance of grabbing a reasonable night's sleep after a wash and opportunity to fill his kettle.

A mile or two later, the road slowed to where a track was visible heading off into the trees. He hung a right and followed it, bouncing left and right on the land's uneven surface.

It was fifty yards later that the headlights fell on what appeared to be a building – as solid and imposing-looking a place as he'd spotted since leaving town – standing directly in his path, peering back at him from a clearing in the trees. He stopped, his hands dropping instantly from the wheel.

Whether the place was habited was, at this point, impossible to say. Having been expressly forbidden from having any contact with members of the local population it would be a foolhardy act to go banging on the door at this hour simply to clarify the situation one way or the other.

But it warranted a moment's thought. If the place did turn out to be occupied maybe he'd get a chance to fill up his kettle, stretch his legs and get a bit of warmth. And maybe even get a bite of something to eat beyond a few dehydrated lumps in a mug of boiling water.

It was at that moment that a face, or what appeared to be a face – appeared at one of the upper windows. Kember instantly retreated, knowing to keep himself anonymous at all times and in all circumstances.

He looked again. Seconds later, he or she, was back – a small moon-like head peering at him and then quickly vanishing, showing no more desire to be spotted than had Kember.

For all the warnings and reminders of being a foreigner in this most hostile of environments – sitting in his car at the dead of night, looking out on the sort of place that might have been lifted from a kid's story-book, there'd surely be little harm in doing a bit of investigating. If only to discover what kind of an establishment he'd stumbled onto: house, barn or some kind of hostel from the look of it. Which, for the time being, wasn't really the issue. It was a building, a place with walls and maybe indoor heating. Chance to maybe get a decent wash if nothing else.

Easing his way toward the right corner of the building he stepped from the car, closing the door behind him.

Mi Yung had been backed against the wall for some time. Though no stranger to fear this wasn't the kind of fear she'd come to expect. A fear of authority was one thing: a part and parcel of life during her early years in town, but having it spring from strange looking vehicles at the dead of night was a different proposition altogether. The first interruption to her routine – day or night – in all the years she'd been there. The only explanation she could come up with...a member of the local *imminban*: a people's vigilantes group – seeking to catch her off her guard by arriving when least expected.

Hands backed against the wall, she could do little but wait, and hope.

Having knocked and got little response Kember had been surprised to feel the doorknob turn so easily. He pushed it open and peered inside. A narrow flight of stairs faced him. He stood a moment, not wanting to be construed as a trespasser, or worse still – an intruder on some family's evening meal.

Mi Yung had heard noises but knew it wasn't her place to set about investigating them. A fear had taken such a grip as she hadn't experienced since hearing the sound of feet on the stairs at home all those years ago: fear followed by a door bursting open, and then voices, rapidly becoming cries, more feet, more voices...too many people crammed into such a confined space – and then silence...

When footsteps sounded and the door opened at the far end of the room, she stiffened and had no way of stifling a cry.

Kember was intrigued but not yet unduly disturbed. He still had no way of knowing what kind of a place he'd stumbled into and the opportunity to venture a little further didn't seem beyond him.

It was on spotting the figure at the end of the room that he stopped – knowing first and foremost to keep calm and make no gesture that might be construed as threatening; offering nothing beyond the brief raising of a hand and a quick 'hi'.

First impression was of looking into the face of a child though it was difficult to be sure. Again he raised a hand. There was a movement across the floor.

Though no way near up to conversing in the language, the suggestion before embarking on his trip that he arm himself with a few words and phrases – simple introductions and a few questions that could be answered with a nod or quick 'yes' or 'no' – had been heeded. And at this moment seemed about the best advice he'd been given. He tried a few words and then stopped.

Mi Yung wasn't quite so terrified as she'd been moments earlier. The man bore no resemblance to a soldier or the police or one of the Party's agents as far as she could recall – though it was difficult to be sure who or what he resembled at that distance.

Kember had established that he was in the company of a young female. How young was difficult to gauge, it being difficult to gauge the age of anyone in this land, particularly their females. He took another shot at a simple greeting, speaking deliberately slowly and keeping an eye for the first hint of a reaction. The possibility of other occupants waiting in the wings hadn't escaped him though, on first impression, seemed unlikely. He tried a few more words – his name and an attempt to briefly put her in the picture.

There was a movement opposite. He thought it might be a smile but he couldn't be sure. He tried a bit more, dutifully avoiding any reference to his nationality.

Mi Yung watched, unable to comprehend what was happening, or worse still – what might be about to happen over the next few minutes. Most of what the man was saying and the way he was viewing her suggested he didn't mean her any harm, at least not yet. But she was still struck by it being such an untimely intrusion, and by one so odd looking.

Not having set eyes on a fellow human-being for some years, her recollections of 'people' were rapidly fading, but what images remained bore scant resemblance to the man stood before her at that moment: such a huge nose and huge eyes rather like the eyes of a small calf. And such scruffy clothes. Her only explanation – a 'party official' in disguise...

one of a cadre of men and women whose job was to pursue domestic breaches of the peace as opposed to more serious cases of law-breaking. Though never having seen any of these people in the flesh, it was difficult to say.

Another possibility – one that even at this time of day she wasn't entirely dismissing – that *the* moment, designated by the Dearest Leader, had finally arrived! The moment, after all these years, when she would be called upon to fulfil her duties as coffee and tea provider for an unnamed, unexpected and most honoured guest.

She reached for the two canisters, thrusting them aloft like a pair of sporting trophies...

'Tea'?...'Coffee' ? The words delivered in her most well-rehearsed voice.

Kember was impressed. A cup of coffee would go down well after the drama of the last few minutes. He opted for 'coffee', nodding to help convey the impression they were hopefully operating on the same wavelength.

It was greeted with an immediate filling of the kettle and a babble of vocabulary that could have eased or worsened his immediate prospects without a clue as to which it might be.

Wearing her hugest smile the cup was handed to him – along with an obligatory bow of the head, a bow returned by her guest. After which Mi Yung turned to the counter to take a tray of what appeared to be berries. Kember took a small cluster of berries from the tray, making a show of chewing enthusiastically.

Quite what was going on here he couldn't imagine: a girl – in some ways little more than a child – stuck in the middle of nowhere with apparent sole responsibility for running whatever establishment it was. Maybe some 'Youth Opportunities' project or Rehabilitation-Centre, though it was hard to imagine the kid staring wide-eyed at him slotting into any such role. But there was little point in puzzling over such things for too long. He needed to keep an eye on the time and remember his prime purpose in stopping – to top up his flask, hopefully grab a decent wash and stretch his legs a little before setting off to find his spot for the night.

After the coffee – that didn't quite taste like coffee but given the circumstances, was close enough – it was back to the dessert tray. Kember took a few berries, patting his stomach as indication he could cope with little more of her hospitality on that score – a gesture that met some amusement behind the counter. They tasted grainy and slightly sweet but were palatable enough with a dash of what remained of his coffee.

Whatever the circumstances she was undoubtedly alone. Beyond which there was little to speculate over. Kember finished his coffee and looked round for signs of a washroom, rubbing hands and face as indication of his intent.

In an instant Mi Yung was off the stool, guiding him to a small room where he found a basin and toilet – flush variety too, something of a bonus in these parts one would imagine.

Ablutions behind him he had an eye on his watch and was soon making indications of needing to get back on the road.

It was seeing her face drop that stopped him a moment – his arrival on the scene appearing to have touched a nerve.

'Mi...' the girl was saying, pointing at herself. Kember nodded.

'Yes...'you'...'you'...'

'Mi...' she said again, repeating the word and then 'Yung'...'Mi Yung'.

The penny dropped, it was Kember's turn to smile.

'Mi Yung..' he said, deliberately repeating the line. 'Mi Yung... . .Steve,' he said, pointing at himself and repeating the word.

'Ste-ve...' Mi Yung chanted, repeating the word twice, three times, and breaking into another smile.

With the introductions behind them, Kember took another check on the surroundings. The room was long and narrow with a counter at one end and a line of chairs stacked against a rear wall. In the furthest corner was what at first appeared to be a dining table but – on closer viewing – turned out to be a pool table!

'Pool,' he said, pointing and making his way towards the rear of the room.

'Pool!' Mi Yung repeated, following his steps, as eager as ever to be seen fulfilling her role as hostess.

From time to time Mi Yung would amuse herself playing a game of rolling the balls back and forth playing bounce with the different colours and striking them against the cushion with the long stick. But she had no further knowledge of how things were supposed to be or how or why the table had been put there other than to provide moments of amusement. One step ahead of her, Kember was already at the table, looking over his shoulder to check his interrupting the arrangement of the balls wasn't going to cause offence.

'Pool!' Mi Yung repeated, full of smiles, watching Kember arrange the balls in a pattern, take the stick and lower himself to take aim, levelling it across the table and striking a few of the balls, making them ricochet against the side and with such force she could visualise them bouncing off and rolling across the floor. Watching as he strode round the table and bent again at the waist to hammer-home a quick succession of pockets. An outbreak of clapping followed. Kember looked up.

'Okay?' he said, bowing.

'Okay!' Mi Yung repeated, returning the bow.

'Your turn,' he said.

'Your turn,' Mi Yung sang back. Trying not to appear too showy he pocketed another brace before handing her the cue, insisting she took it after demonstrating how to make a rest for the cue with one hand and take aim by lowering her eye to table level, offering a little encouragement when, at first attempt, the first balls went scattering in all directions. But she wasn't an entire novice at these things and was able to grasp the technique required to have the balls cannon off each other in roughly the intended direction, soon managing to slot a few, aided by a voice of encouragement from over her shoulder. He tried explaining the rules: showing her the spots and colours and idea of delaying pocketing the black. She kind of got it, sufficient to pass a half hour or so and not be too taken in when Kember popped a few concessionary pockets on her behalf.

It was in acknowledgement of her success and hospitality, that Kember remembered the bottles of wine and crates of beer he'd brought with him to liven up his evenings on setting up camp for the night. Attempting to communicate his intentions he backed to the door and made his way downstairs. Mi Yung had no way grasped what he had said but something in his manner suggested he wasn't disappearing for good, confirmed minutes later, when he reappeared armed with a few crates.

The counter was to be their base. It was down to Mi Yung to provide suitable receptacles, producing two mugs from beneath the counter. She watched as he popped a top off one of the bottles. The wine was cheap and likely a little on the rancid side but it would suffice. Mi Yung took each bottle in hand, peering curiously at what she could make of each label and breaking into another of her little smiles.

She helped with the pouring, impressed by the wine's distinctive blackcurrant aroma. Only when Kember had taken his can and raised it to view did she respond by taking a sip from her cup, curling her face and looking away to hide her initial lack of enthusiasm. It was on the second and third sip that its bitterness relented a fraction, and by the fourth and fifth seemed barely an issue.

She was no less impressed by the sound of the ring-can being pulled and the foaming effect it produced, watching him pour the frothy contents into a cup.

'Beer,' he explained, holding the cup aloft.

'Beer!' she repeated, reaching for her own cup and drinking more eagerly.

'Wine,' he explained, nodding at her cup and raising the bottle to view.

'Wine!' she repeated, laughing.

It called for a little entertainment: a timely introduction to Western rock music courtesy of the CD player which had been put to one side while he tended to the drinks. Putting his cup on the counter he turned to the machine he'd brought from the car, taking a handful of CD's and raising each to view. The only music Mi Yung had ever heard had been children's choirs in school and the thousand strong choruses in the Dearest Leader's birthday celebrations in her early years.

Kember searched the pile carefully selected from his shelf at home before taking what seemed as good an introduction as any from its shield, the small silver disc held to view.

"The Rolling Stones'...' he explained, doing a quick check on the album's details.

'Rolling...Stones!' Mi Yung repeated, eyeing the cover and making every effort to be seen taking in some of its information, watching as he fiddled around with the machine and placed it on the counter.

"Sixties r&b...' he explained. 'Pop/r&b.'

'Pop/r&b...' she sang back, taking hold of the CD case, checking out its decorative features whilst standing back to watch Kember adjust the knobs and then retreat a few steps.

A laugh followed from over his shoulder, then another as the introduction of guitar chords and a thumping drum beat spilled out of the speakers. Kember reached for his drink, tapping his foot as demonstration of how to 'get into the groove' of these things.

For Mi Yung the whole evening was turning into something quite surreal, governed by circumstances she neither understood nor – by this stage – felt it was her place to understand. The man's appearance – his strange looks and strange music blaring from a strange-looking machine was evidently the order of the day and, she presumed, was to be greeted with such cooperation as was her place to provide.

Such sounds she'd never encountered before, an odd thumping sound like marching feet or an approaching train.

Buoyed by the wine and beginning to warm to the rhythms,

it was back for another round of pool – Mi Yung opting to arrange the balls and recalling Kember's instructions from earlier, firing off a few cannon-like openers, a few of which came close to sinking in the pockets.

Over several games they worked their way through early Dylan, Bruce Springsteen and The Best Of Johnny Cash, to the accompaniment of several cans of beer and significant inroads into a second bottle of wine.

How things were to progress from there was very much in the balance. The idea of hitting the road at such an hour and after several beers didn't appeal and Kember was hoping he'd be offered a corner where he could pitch his sleeping bag and maybe get a little shut eye.

All of which – from his host's point of view – was for later. This was *her* party, or it had become *her* party, and she was resolved to milking every last drop from it. The second bottle was still over half full – and with the berries finally reduced to a few stalks she turned her attention back to the CD sleeves.

'You choose,' Kember said, nodding at the pile of lids clutched in her hand.

'You choose!' Mi Yung repeated, presenting each case for Kember's inspection.

'Your choice,' he said again. There was a flicker of recognition as a case was turned to view – the case that had got the evening off in some style at what now seemed an age ago.

'Stones...!' she announced, extending the case for Kember's approval.

Kember obligingly took the disc and fitted it into the slot, its opening bars signalling recollections of an hour or so earlier.

'*I can't get no...*' She had a technique for keeping time and breaking into her own foot-tapping routine.

'*Sat-is-fac-tion...*' Kember repeated, an arm thumping the air in imitation of John Travolta's late 70's on-screen antics, instantly picked up by Mi Yung who first placed herself behind

Kember to mirror his movements and later insisted on swapping places – taking her turn at the front.

With Mi Yung in pole-position and Kember happy to slot into whatever direction the evening took them – a sudden lurch to his left was accompanied by an even more dramatic thrust of his arm....

A combination of which brought a clenched fist firmly into contact with the portrait of Dearest Leader – releasing him from its hook and sending him tumbling to the ground, where – with a resounding crack – he came to rest at the foot of the wall.

Kember stopped instantly, unlike Mi Yung who – with her back to him – continued to jig merrily, blissfully unaware of developments a few feet behind her.

The sounds continued to blare out as Kember quickly knelt to take the frame from the floor, giving it a quick brush-down and eyeing a small crack running the entire width of the glass.

And take a moment to consider his next move – aware that this was *not* like dropping a family photograph back at home. One of the few facts he'd managed to glean about the place before embarking on his trip – that defiling any image of the land's near god-like leader was an act tantamount to treason.

Back to his feet in seconds he reached up to hook the picture back into place. Standing back to view it from a few paces away, the crack was barely visible, but on any closer inspection would be as evident as Mi Yung continuing to dance the night away a few feet ahead of him.

He needed to think – the absurdity of the situation, for now, neither here nor there. What was done was done. The only thing that mattered was what was to *be* done.

The easy option would be to disappear off the scene first thing in the morning, knowing he'd be off-the-hook the minute he stepped into his car.

But standing in the midst of everything still going on just a few feet away, the idea was swiftly dismissed. The fact remained that the whole evening: from turning up uninvited on her doorstep, bearing bottles of wine, cans of beer, music...

was ultimately down to him. In effect taking advantage of a situation he had no business expecting – let alone exploiting – simply on the grounds of it appearing to be the highlight of her year.

One thing in his favour was that she'd remained totally unaware of what had happened, and – as such – had no immediate cause to panic. His immediate priority – to bring the evening to as swift and uneventful a conclusion as possible, ideally over a final game of pool so as to put a bit of distance between them and the picture.

His plan – convened whilst setting up the balls on the table and admittedly in the midst of an alcoholic fog – was to rise early and drive until he found a shop or what passed as a shop, where he might be able to buy a suitable frame, or even another picture that could be substituted for the one he had defaced. Pictures of the guy were everywhere and finding or buying a replacement surely wouldn't be an impossible task. Sizes tended to be uniform, and there was a small border round the original image that would stand a few centimetres leeway if necessary. Another possibility was finding a picture on the wall of some building, preferably uninhabited, that he could either steal or possibly buy and replace with Mi Yung's, or just use its frame. One thing he had a relative abundance of was money – one thing folk round these parts could certainly do with – of whatever denomination.

With a tale at hand to explain his early departure, he'd attempted to grab what sleep he could – at one point considering putting her in the picture (so to speak) about what had happened and with regard to his plan. The point being she'd be able to advise him on the best route to take in acquiring the pane or frame or replacing the picture. Maybe even producing another picture from a cellar or somewhere beneath the stairs. But – aside from its implications, the language would be an issue. No way could he communicate anything in such detail as that. And the possibility of reducing her to a state of panic was too big a price to pay. He would stick to his plan.

If travelling by day was a bleak experience, doing so at the crack of dawn was like riding rough-shod over someone's death-bed. After an hour of spotting little beyond barren fields and a few military-looking outposts it was time to draw to a halt; chance to take a drink of water and give his plan a little more thought.

He knew he needed to keep a steady head, reminding himself that the only concern at this point was the likelihood of someone – police, army or whoever was employed for such tasks – bursting in on Mi Yung in his absence. How often checks were made in such remote parts was anybody's guess – probably not very. Which only served to compound the problem: whether to gamble on time being in his favour; a gamble neither he nor Mi Yung could afford to lose.

Equally concerning was the prospect of Mi Yung waking to discover his parting shot: that having accepted her hospitality, he'd wilfully turned it on its head, leaving her to pick up the pieces – hardly the kind of memory he was seeking to accompany him on the journey home.

He decided to give it another thirty minutes, fifteen of which was sufficient to confirm the fact he was wasting his time. That the likelihood of stumbling across anywhere even resembling a shop or a building that could be investigated was about as likely as stumbling across the man himself.

Drawing to a halt he needed to re-think the whole thing; frustration rapidly turning to irritation at finding himself in the midst of the kind of farce that ultimately had nothing to do with him, or *ought* to have nothing to do with him.

Equally frustrating to know that, for now at least, that wasn't even the issue. What he needed to do was to stop thinking and get driving and – if only to bring a moment's reprieve – consider the possibility that even in Mickey Mouse countries like this people might accept the fact that accidents can happen. That on his return she'd dash up to him, telling him not to be so stupid, that the whole thing was in hand.

Leaning on the wheel, he headed back in the direction from whence he'd come.

It was close to midday that the turning and familiar line of trees slowed him to take the bend just a hundred yards or so from Mi Yung's place.

It was even quieter than he'd remembered it. He nursed the car another twenty yards before drawing to a halt and peering up at the window expecting – or hoping – to see a small moon-like face peering back at him but spotting nothing.

Leaving the car in the same spot as before, he approached the door. It was open. He eased it wide and peered in. The place was in darkness. He thought of calling out but something warned against doing anything quite so rash. Instead he made his way up the stairs, still half expecting to find Mi Yung at the counter. The place was cold and empty – a marked contrast to the mood of the previous evening. He strolled from room to room, calling after her, wanting to get a reply, if only to hear a voice. Checking the sleeping room next door.

It took little more than a minute to confirm the whole place, upstairs and down, was deserted. He checked the wall. The picture was still there, a tiny crack running the full width of its lower quarter.

He retraced his steps, running over a few possibilities: that she'd gone for a stroll, collecting berries for the tray. That she'd be back shortly and he just needed to wait. But somehow it seemed a long shot; a more viable explanation already looming: that checks were made more often than he'd imagined or that on discovering his parting-shot she'd made a rapid exit. He looked round, checking for a note that might have been left on the counter or on the pool table – equally unlikely given the language issue.

He reached beneath the counter, checking the two canisters. Tea, coffee, the can of dehydrated milk – all sitting there waiting to be called into action at a moment's notice. To his left – two empty wine bottles and crumpled ring-pull cans alongside two cups sitting by the sink.

He made his way to the door. He'd give it twenty minutes. He'd toyed with leaving a note of his own but to what effect? What was he going to write? A few words of a language he barely knew. And where exactly would that leave him?

A minute later he was back in his car.

And five minutes after that he put the car into gear and headed off down the track, hitting the tarmac shortly after.

Leaning more firmly on the wheel he contemplated putting a CD on the player but could barely summon the energy to do so.

Instead, he put his foot down. His only concern – to find a parking spot close enough to running water, chance to grab a wash and fill his kettle for the night to come.

* * * * *

Post Script:

Having woken in a state of total confusion and such a headache as she'd never experienced before, Mi Yung's first task – having attempted to piece together the events of the previous evening – was to get outside and get a little air into her lungs.

All she'd been able to recall was that the man *Steve ...if* that was his real name – had been on some kind of assignment and had sought somewhere to relax after all the driving.

The walk had helped relieve the headache and nauseous feeling in her stomach that had been with her since she'd awoken. And allowed her to replenish her supply of berries, the previous evening having seen off her current stock. The berries were plentiful enough but involved a lengthy hike into the forest to gather sufficient quantities.

It was on her return close to one-o-clock that she had set about her duties.

And whilst smoothing the cloth down the Dearest Leader's picture that she was surprised to feel the cloth snag against some interference and then dismayed to discover a jagged line running the width of the picture close to the bottom of the frame...the anxieties prompted by Kember's appearance resurfacing – but with such force she'd barely imagined possible only seconds ago.

With the evening little more than a vague recollection but knowing she'd drunk far too much wine, there could only be one explanation: at some point she must have reached up, jumped up – or done something equally outrageous, and in so doing, struck the picture, reducing it to the abomination now facing her.

In light of which, Kember's departure – in retrospect all so sudden and accompanied by an equally hasty explanation – was clear enough. He'd likely spotted the defiled picture on the floor, immediately putting it back in place to avoid it receiving further attention. And on waking, would have quickly leapt to his responsibilities – setting off to report the incident to the appropriate authorities without delay.

How long it would take the police or party-member or whoever was assigned to such tasks to arrive was anybody's guess. In all the years she'd been there she'd never had a single visit from anyone. But it seemed all that was about to change; that it was simply a matter of time...hours possibly, before officials would descend, quite likely in droves – and Mi Yung's world would be once again thrust into an irreversible downward spiral – with, on this occasion, little means of escape.

Adding to her frustration was knowing a spare picture existed in the cellar, smuggled secretly into her case by a family member on vacating their apartment back in town in the event of an accident such as this occurring! That it was somewhere at the back of the cellar and could easily be recovered and removed from its protective towel to take its place on the wall.

But sadly, she knew that was no longer the issue.

For whoever he was and whatever authority he would bring to bear, Kember had witnessed the crime first hand – the hurried explanation of his departure making far more sense now than at the time. Aware that failure to report the incident without delay would make him equally culpable.

Her dilemma was clear: to replace the picture knowing that it could be construed as an attempt to deceive the authorities: to give the impression nothing had happened when first hand evidence was to the contrary – or to leave the picture in full view in the hope that her honesty might reap some reward; that with a replacement at hand and evidence pointing to the fact that over the years she'd attempted to fulfil her duties as one of Dearest Leader's children with the utmost loyalty and devotion – the police or party members might find it in them to accept the fact that even in such remote parts as this – accidents can happen.

On thinking about it further – hardly a gamble at all. The damage was done; an attempt to convey the impression it hadn't – as stupid as leaping in the air to dislodge the picture in the first place...

For better or worse – the picture would remain exactly where it was.

With the weight of what responsibility remained resting heavily on her shoulders, she set about her first duty of the day – to clean up the mess from the previous evening – before turning to give the two canisters a shake. In so doing, barely giving the picture a glance – possibly an attempt (and maybe succeeding) to convince herself that The Man himself...The Dearest Leader, didn't exist – and never would.

Taking a seat on the stool she spooned the gruel into a mix and fed herself with it, drawing her smock around her to help keep out the chill.

From now on it was simply a question of waiting.

Note: The story is based on an incident recorded around 2013 when a young woman/girl was kept in isolation and 'employed' to sell tea and coffee to almost non-existent visitors to a remote area of North Korea. On one occasion she was visited by an American tourist/visitor who, amongst other things, enjoyed a game of pool with her. Whether she still exists or her 'position of employment' still exists I know not.

Additional note – In no way is the story an attempt to present a historically or politically accurate picture. A number of features/scenarios may well be entirely implausible, unrealistic or simply incorrect in a modern-day context.

In which case – regard the setting as an imaginary land bearing a passing resemblance to NK.

* The Title 'Dearest' Leader...the word used to describe the North Korean Leader varies from one dynasty to another: 'Dear' generally acknowledged as an opening prefix, from which 'Dear' and 'Dearest' (my interpretation) stems.

The Curious Incident Of
The Writer In The Afternoon

[A sequel to 'The Curious Incident Of The Writer At Night Time' featured in the collection...'Telling Tales'.]

It was another uneventful afternoon in the study of Bacup Lawrence where, twixt the hours of six am. and midnight and, as ever, surrounded by the artefacts and accoutrements of a past life...his father's past life...his grandfather's past life – their man was to be seen pacing the room in a state of some anxiety, to all intents a spent force in his mission to make sense of an increasingly complex world.

'What's he about?' asked Toy Trumpet stirring himself to observe their chap stalking hither and thither in a state of considerable agitation.

'Searching for inspiration,' whispered Arnold – the long droopy snake, designed to keep the draught from creeping under the door on those long winter evenings – content to observe their man from a distance whilst attempting to keep everyone amused by repeatedly tying himself in knots and swiftly disengaging himself Houdini-style.

'Ideas!' came the cry from below where their man – by this stage an author of no mean repute – was to be seen prowling this way and that, drinking coffee and smoking incessantly. And staring hard at the scene beyond the window: the garden's greens and pinks registering only as a blank featureless canvas awaiting the onslaught of the artist's brush.

'Ideas!' he cried. 'Give me work! I am the seed from which the sapling grows.'

'What's he about?' asked Pencil-Sharpener, doing a few quick turns on the edge of the desk in an attempt to attract the attention of one of Lawrence's latest acquisitions – a rather attractive pot figurine ballet-dancer caught mid-stride in one of her more provocative moves.

'Searching for the spark that might ignite the fire of creativity,' explained Lab-Top, slotting the last piece of his solitaire game into place and examining the fruits of his labour with a wry smile.

'Leave it out Lab-Top,' came the cry from all sides.

'What do you know about 'fires of creativity?' 'You are but a cold inanimate object having no part to play in the creative process...'

'Dealing with *real* feeling and *real* people.'

Even Shakespeare – usually as quick off the mark as anyone once the barbs were flying – remained strangely subdued, himself more than aware that a writer's lot is frequently anything but a happy one.

It was down to Arnold busily untangling himself from his latest party trick to lend his voice to the discussion, directing his comment to Plastic-Gnome a few inches along the shelf.

'Well – I have to say I think there's something in what LT says,' he said. 'For a writer devoid of ideas is like an elephant devoid of a trunk. Isn't that right Pot-Elephant?'

Pot-Elephant nodded grimly.

'Or a Toy-Trumpet short of a tune,' said Plastic-Gnome, attempting to shield his ears from the cacophonous racket threatening to blow them all away at the far end of the shelf – Toy Trumpet in the midst of yet another improvised jazz routine – his contortions close to fever-pitch in acknowledgement of recent ventures into more funk-orientated arrangements.

'Only the jazz-man speaks directly from the soul,' he cried, fingers schlepping up and down the scales as an expression of his inner hurt.

It was as if to bring a halt to the squabbling that a flurry of arms beneath gave way to a hail of manuscripts soon to be seen flying in all directions, a number of which floated in the air before coming to land on the shelf beside them.

'What have we here?' said Arnold reaching for one of the sheets and casting a miniscule eye over its hurriedly scribbled contents.

Placing himself to one side for a second Toy-Trumpet seized a handful of sheets to give their contents a quick shufti.

'Evidently the blurbs of some current novelists' work,' he said, reading from a few and following each word with a plastic mouthpiece.

'A tale of revenge and redemption set against a background of sibling rivalry...'

There were looks from various quarters of the shelf, Tiny-Troll seizing another of the sheets in a thimble-size fist to cast an eye over its contents. *'A couple in 40's rural England caught in a tug-of-war fuelled by jealousy and false promises...'*

Plastic-Gnome too was quick to join the party, snatching at one of the sheets slowly coming to rest in his lap.

'A New England couple struggling to come to terms with the pain of a fragmented past___'

'Dear me,' said Pot-Elephant with a shake of his head, peering over PG's shoulder to avoid having to leaf through the sheets of his own accord. 'What turgid waters our chaps are obliged to tread.'

'Is there any end to the pain that might yet drive our men to distraction?' cried Lab-Top, his lid flapping repeatedly in sympathy with the writer's plight.

'Shut up Lab-Top,' came the cry.

'What do you know about 'men's distractions'?'

'The only thing driving anyone to distraction round here is you!'

'What do you reckon Shakespeare?' asked Pencil-Sharpener doing a few more turns on the side of the desk and eyeing the great man perched imperiously on his marble plinth. As was often the case…'no answer' was the only audible reply from above – the voice of a man himself no stranger to the angst that is the lot of many a man's creative spirit.

'There's more,' cried Plastic-Gnome, plucking another sheet from the air and scanning its contents with a quizzical eye. '*A vivid portrait of family life in the wake of the post-war American psyche'…Short-listed for the Man-Booker Prize.*"… There were pulled faces, the sheet sent spinning to the floor to the accompaniment of such a rip-roaring fart from Chaucer as had each and every one of them assured a thunderclappe must have erupted in the very skies above them.

There were guffaws and much to-and-froing along every inch of the shelf.

Only Shakespeare was staying out of it, sufficiently knowledgeable to avoid being drawn into discussions on such matters as prizes, short-lists for prizes, monthly competitions and the like.

'Bah humbug___' he was heard to cry – as ever, a good few years ahead of his time. 'For what is an artist if not a man or woman engaged in a pursuit thankfully devoid of such notions as winners and losers?'

Though – as was often the case with The Great Man – whether anyone was listening was an entirely different issue.

'What do you reckon Chaucer?' said Tiny-Troll, deliberately directing his question to one who undoubtedly knew a thing or two about telling a tale – and whose response was yet another rip-roaring fart threatening to blow them away over and above Toy-Trumpet's remonstrations a few minutes previous.

Which, as luck, or arguably fate, would have it, was – it seemed – the very spark to ignite the creative spirit for too long left simmering in their midst: their man in an instant back at his desk – an A4 sheet seized from the pile and stuffed ecstatically into the typewriting machine.

'Aha…' came the cry.

'Action!' announced Toy-Trumpet.

'The burst of inspiration that is meat and drink to our man's survival!'

'Of what does our fellow write?' asked Tiny-Troll shuffling closer to get in on the act and directing his question to Pencil-Eraser who was close enough to follow proceedings word by word.

'Likely that thing about *love being the thing we all crave for, yet – so often – the catalyst for disenchantment and despair,*' said Lab-Top somewhat sulkily at once again being overlooked when it came to getting down the all-important first draft. 'Was it Saul Bellow who said...*Though I love only where I have lived, I live only where I never seemed to have loved...?*'

'Shut up Lab-Top. What do you know about 'love'?'

'Or about where people live?'

'Or what they crave for?'

'The only source of disenchantment and despair round here is you!'

At which point – silence fell, as did the questions: to a man as redundant as they were once the meat and drink of their people's day.

For who is this man who suddenly toils at his desk like the blacksmith hammering away at his anvil?

He is a writer...

'Just a guy trying to make sense of the world around him,' said Toy-Trumpet.

'Or relating to the world around him,' said Plastic-Gnome.

'Or – a man *embarking on a journey that might yet turn out to be an engaging metaphor for the lifelong search for the inner self,*' said Lab-Top.

'Shut up Lab-Top,' they all said.

'What do you know about engaging metaphors?'

'Or the life-long search for the inner-self?'

'For you are but a_____'

* * * * *

The Man Who Was His Own Man

Ardcock was – and always had been – his own man. He did his own thing, in which respect he was disinclined to justify himself.

At the greengrocers, as in other shops he frequented, he stood waiting patiently in the queue, showing neither frustration nor impatience that the queue was taking a good deal longer than expected getting him to the cash-till on account of an elderly woman struggling with the coins in her purse. She was being helped by the cashier – a handsome woman in a dark blue top, awarded a fleeting glance from Ardcock but nothing more.

When the woman behind him in the queue dropped a tangerine on the floor due to it being cradled in her arms instead of put in a basket he watched but made no move to pick it up. She wasn't elderly so was presumably capable of picking it up herself. Plus – picking it up for her might be viewed as being patronising – like he was assuming she was incapable of picking it up.

Only when a second tangerine slipped from her grasp and went rolling across the floor did he step in, thinking she might be able to cope with one tangerine dropping on the floor but two would be a bit tricky seeing as she had another three tangerines nestling in the crook of her arm. His thinking – whilst leaning to rescue one tangerine from the floor was that he might just as well grab them both. Which was what he did – placing both in the crook of her arm as he returned to his place in the queue.

The woman thanked him profusely but he thought little of it. It wasn't necessarily an act of kindness, just what seemed appropriate under the circumstances. Before long the queue was moving and his thoughts were only on getting closer to the till.

'Careless of me,' the woman said. Ardcock nodded but was disinclined to comment further on the grounds that it could come across as being flippant or possibly facetious – neither of which he had any inclination to be.

'Butter fingers,' she said. 'All fingers and thumbs.'

The queue was down to one person. He had his wallet in his right hand pocket and his purse in the other pocket.

The payment for his goods went smoothly and he left the shop pausing only to check the cost of new potatoes which he found from experience tended to vary in quality ie. taste. He was at the point of leaving the shop when the woman with the tangerines bumped into him whilst putting her change in her purse.

She apologised profusely.

The pair left the shop, turning right at the top of the road, both walking at a similar pace. The woman spoke to him twice: once saying it was a nice day the other telling him she liked the street they were walking along.

Ardcock looked both sides of the road. He neither liked nor disliked the street, any more than he liked nor disliked the town. It was where he happened to live and, as such, was content to leave it at that.

Though having the option of disappearing into any of the shops they were passing, he didn't. He was heading for the sea-front and had little reason to change his agenda on account of being accompanied by someone whose tangerines he'd rescued from the floor of the greengrocers. On arrival at the sea-front his plan was to turn right. Whether the woman planned to do the same remained to be seen.

Reaching the point where the High Street met the promenade the woman said she was going for a cup of coffee.

Ardcock looked at his watch. It was four-thirty, round about the time he often took a cup of coffee himself. He could say he was going for a coffee too, or he could avoid saying anything and make his departure.

'I'd like to buy you a coffee,' the woman said. 'Because you helped me in the greengrocers and I appreciated it.' Ardcock considered the offer, which was a generous one if not really necessary and one he felt little compulsion to take her up on – or turn down.

'Okay.' He'd made his decision. He'd quite like a coffee and saw no reason not to take her up on the offer.

The café was as much a restaurant as a café. An Italian place with a huge purple awning that appeared to specialise in ice-cream. The waiter was polite and welcoming, pulling their chairs out for them to take their seats. The woman had her bag close to her possibly so no-one could run off with it. Ardcock had his wallet in his inside pocket for easy access.

She asked him his preference when it came to coffee. He considered the question. 'Latte'. She said she liked 'Americana' but not always.

When the waiter arrived she ordered a 'regular coffee'. He ordered a 'latte'.

Waiting for the coffee Ardcock was thinking. The offer to buy him a coffee had come out of the blue. It could be a gesture of politeness or it could be that she was seeking a little company. Which could mean she had designs on getting to know him with a view to possibly striking up a relationship. Which could mean one of two things: friendship or a romantic relationship.

First impressions were the woman appeared to be the sociable sort which – at that point – was neither here nor there. She'd been checking the menu, not necessarily because she was planning to order something but more as a means of occupying herself.

'They do nice ice-creams here.' Ardcock was listening even though he rarely ate ice-cream. The observation made him wonder if she had children. Probably not or she wouldn't be sitting drinking coffee with him in a café.

'Anyway – I'm Celia…or Cissy.' She looked him in the eye. Ardcock saw no reason not to disclose his name.

'I'm Ardcock,' he said, half expecting a reaction. People sometimes commented that it was a strange name which maybe it was. She said it was an interesting name. He told her it was his father's and grandfather's name.

She had been scrutinising the ice-cream menu. She put it to one side saying she fancied an ice-cream. Shifting forwards in her seat she offered to buy Ardcock an ice-cream. Buying him an ice-cream would be unnecessary. Picking a few tangerines off the floor was no way the equivalent of buying a cup of coffee *and* an ice-cream but she insisted so he went along with it. He'd fulfilled his obligation – insisting it wasn't necessary but as she'd offered he saw no reason not to take her up on the offer. He opted for a raspberry-ripple when she asked if he had a preference.

It was when she got out of her seat to examine the contents of the ice-cream freezer that he had a chance to view her more closely.

She was a lithe woman with narrow hips, legs that appeared to have kept their shape, showing little sign of fleshing out or sagging beneath the buttocks. Her hair was shoulder length, not always the case with women her age. The waiter told her he would bring the ice-creams over.

She retook her seat wrestling with something in her bag.

'So…' Shifting menus and serviettes to one side she leant forward on her elbows. With coffee ordered and ice-creams on the way there was the opportunity to to sit back and relax.

She looked to her left then to her right. Then she looked him in the eye.

'So here we are then. I quite like a coffee around this time in the afternoon.' Ardcock was similarly inclined.

'Me too,' he said.

He had noticed the woman's eyes were blue. He rarely noticed the colour of people's eyes. It was one of the things writers of books frequently referred to – but not him. To him, the colour of people's eyes was neither here nor there. As was their complexion, or their expression. He had noticed her breasts were firm and prominent under the light brown top.

'So – do you live locally?'

It was a simple enough question yet could be designed to take one of two directions: routine conversation or conversation geared to them sparking up some kind of relationship. Ardcock considered his response.

'Yes – not far away.'

Shortly after, the ice-creams arrived.

Ardcock decided to return the question. She told him she lived not far from the centre, a short bus ride away, adding a few details about the flat she lived in. Ardcock was listening whilst attempting to spoon ice-cream with an incredibly small ladle on an incredibly long stem. Whether she was making casual conversation or attempting to strike up some kind of relationship, he couldn't be sure and wasn't, at this stage, inclined to dwell on. Either way it warranted a response. He gave her a few facts about where he lived: a two bedroomed flat without a garden about a mile from the town centre.

It was on allowing a few more spoonfuls of ice-cream to pass his lips that he wondered how she'd react to having a few dollops of ice-cream popped on her naked body. Not that he had any plans to put the question. It wasn't the sort of question you could put to someone unless you were in a relationship with them, and even then more likely a *steady* relationship. And, you'd still have to pick your moment and could never be sure whether you'd get a straight answer; that would largely depend on the woman you were asking. Plus – there'd likely be an element of surprise at being asked such a question. It would likely depend on circumstances. Drinking coffee and eating ice-cream in an Italian restaurant was neither the time nor the place.

'Coffee okay?' Ardcock nodded.

With half his ice-cream consumed he was beginning to think ahead. There were two possibilities on leaving the café.

They could part company with the possibility of meeting again, which also had two possibilities: to spark up a casual friendship or something more serious. Or they could part company without agreeing to meet again.

Unlike some people Celia wasn't overly talkative, which Ardcock had no problem with. She talked about the local bus services, the traffic system in the town and Italian food given they were in an Italian restaurant, though she wasn't entirely sure what constituted Italian food aside from pasta.

Ardcock responded on all three issues though he had no strong feelings about any of them. She was reaching the conclusion Ardock was the steady, possibly introverted type who wasn't one for giving much away though she wasn't of a mind to quiz him on it.

What she *had* noticed was that he had the most unremarkable features: eyes, eyebrows, mouth, nose...hair...all slotting into place like an identikit picture frame, the kind of details you'd struggle to describe if ever required to do so. Plus – his face, currently half illuminated by the lights, had a shiny, almost wax-like quality – rather like a character in a Roy Lichtenstein painting Celia concluded – the kind of impression that hit you on first greeting but would likely fail to make any lasting impression.

Which was when she informed him she was going to the art exhibition at the theatre opposite – one of the town's most famous buildings. Ardcock considered what she was saying, seeing it as either a point-of-information or an invitation to join her. He had no strong views or strong feelings when it came to visiting art-exhibitions.

'How about you?' She was fiddling with her purse as she put the question. 'Fancy casting an eye over a few pictures?'

He'd been inside the town's most celebrated building twice: once to get out of the rain during a downpour and once to use the wc facilities that tended to be better than the ones in the High Street.

It was a suggestion that warranted a moment's thought.

'Okay,' he said, spooning what remained of his ice-cream and placing the glass bowl to one side.

Celia seemed pleased at the prospect of someone accompanying her to the exhibition.

'So – let's pay up and go.'

As they left the café Ardcock wondered if a conversation on the subject of art would follow, but it didn't. She took the purse from her bag and informed him she was going to treat him to the entrance fee on the grounds of him having helped her in the greengrocers. Ardcock pointed out that it was unnecessary. That the cost of a cup of coffee, an ice-cream plus the admission to an art exhibition was excessive when all he'd done was pick a few tangerines off the floor. She asked who was counting and Ardcock would say no more. He'd fulfilled his obligation. Beyond which the ball was in her court.

They crossed the road and entered the building. Despite being a singularly ugly building with ugly-looking windows running the length of its upper storey, the entrance area and the bit inside were spacious and quite pleasing on the eye.

The exhibition was called *Dog Chains – Space Helmets – And Other Fragments Of Civilisation*.

It comprised four rooms each painted white with the pictures along each wall positioned approximately two feet above head height. Ardcock observed the layout, casting an eye round all four rooms before joining Celia in Room One.

'What do you think?' she asked.

'Interesting layout,' he said.

They started at room one and then made their way to rooms two, three and four. They weren't alone. There were approximately twenty other people viewing the exhibition.

Ardcock viewed each picture in turn but had little to say. Talking whilst looking at pictures was unnecessary, plus it could be irritating. And – he didn't have anything *to* say. If Celia spoke he'd speak back. They'd looked at four of the pictures before Celia spoke.

'What do you think?'

Ardcock looked again at the pictures. It was a reasonable question and Ardcock gave it a moment before answering.

'Okay.' Which wasn't saying much but at that moment was all it occurred to him to say.

They went onto the next picture...*Ovals And Bricks*: a series of oval shapes arranged in the shape of a woman with a brick wall balanced above her head. Neither Celia nor Ardcock said anything about the picture which is often the way when you look at pictures. Celia moved a little closer to examine part of the picture she couldn't see clearly from where she'd been standing.

'Mmm,' she said, stepping back. 'Interesting.'

Ardcock thought it was kind of interesting, but he wasn't sure what the picture was trying to convey. Which is often the case with pictures; you don't know what they're for, other than to look at. Which some say is exactly the point: 'It's what it means to you – the viewer'. To Ardcock it meant a woman made of ovals lying on her back with a brick wall balanced above her head. Fleetingly, he wondered how Celia would look lying naked on her back with a brick wall balanced above her head.

'What do you think?' she asked.

'Mmm,' he said.

One picture entitled *Dog's Tin Legs* was of a dog with its legs separated from its body, replaced by tin cans. If asked to express an opinion he'd have said it might have been better to put the tin cans on the floor in front of the dog like it was about to eat whatever was in the tin cans – with or without its legs. And possibly award it a pair of spectacles, an observation that might, or might not, be construed as an attempt at humour – which Ardcock knew sometimes went down well on these occasions. But she didn't ask. Instead she went onto the next picture, as did Ardcock.

It was on viewing the last of the pictures that Celia looked at her watch.

Ardcock too had been considering the situation. It was getting late. The afternoon would soon become evening. It seemed there were two possibilities when they left the building. If they didn't part company, at this stage of proceedings it could mean some kind of relationship was in the offing: either a casual relationship or a more serious relationship like they could be on the verge of 'going out' together. Which sounds odd with people their age, or his age certainly, given you usually associate the phrase with teenagers.

Leaving the exhibition and being asked what he'd thought, he'd said the pictures were 'okay', some better than others. Celia appeared to agree.

'So...' she said once they were back on the road opposite the Italian café. 'What now?'

The question deserved an answer. Ardcock considered the question. Whether to part company or not to part company – with the possibility of striking up a relationship: casual or not so casual. Ardcock was inclined to keep his options open.

Celia was looking at her watch.

'If you'd be interested we could go for a bite to eat.' She was looking the length of the street as she spoke. Ardcock gave the proposal some thought. Eating out would save the hassle of eating at home.

It was close to five-thirty. All things considered, eating out wasn't a bad option.

'Okay,' he said, pulling his collar tight.

Celia seemed relieved. Cooking a meal isn't always ideal when you've spent half the afternoon visiting an art exhibition.

'So – what do you fancy?' She was eyeing him now, waiting to see where he suggested they eat.

Ardcock was thinking. They wouldn't want to go too far which meant eating in the town. Which, as far as he knew, meant one of possibly three or four options: Indian restaurant, Chinese restaurant, Italian restaurant or fish and chips.

'I'm easy,' he said. She drew her coat round her.

'Me too, though I am rather partial to Indian.' She looked to see how the comment had gone down. Indian had come under the radar as one of the options available. He too was partial to Indian food and since she'd come up with the suggestion, why not go along with it?

'Okay.'

The walk to the restaurant would take twenty minutes, which would mean twenty-five minutes if they walked more slowly than they'd walked from the greengrocers. Which meant they'd arrive at the restaurant at around six-o-clock. She came up with a few ideas about what she might like to eat. Ardcock would delay his decision until they were in the restaurant.

The restaurant was called *The Taj Mahal* and played Indian music when you entered. They took the second table on the left and on taking their seats reached for the menus the waiter had handed them. The thing about Indian restaurants is you could eat nearly everything on the menu, but you can't. You have to make a choice which makes it a less than straightforward decision.

'I can never make my mind up.' Celia was back to *The Chef's Specials* on the front cover. As far as Ardcock was concerned there were two possibilities. He weighed the pros and cons of each before making a decision.

It was whilst deciding which of his two shortlisted options to go for that Celia leant towards him. For a moment he thought she was going to offer to pay for his meal which, taking all things into account, would have been inappropriate. But she said she wanted to pay for the drinks as a token of thanks. Which, though still inappropriate, Ardcock chose not to dispute. He'd done his bit. She shook her head and said 'who's counting?' They ordered food and Ardcock ordered a pint of Cobra beer. When she asked if he liked spicy food he said 'kind of'. Which was why he'd ordered a Dhansak which, on past experience, was kind of spicy but too spicy. She'd ordered a chicken korma, saying how she went for taste and hot food was sometimes a bit *too* hot.

There were no issues with the food and they took approximately twenty-five minutes eating it.

They had coffee which Celia insisted on paying for on account of it coming under the 'drinks' heading. Ardcock repeated the point from earlier but left it at that.

He dabbed his lip with a serviette and looked at his watch. Time was getting on.

On leaving the restaurant there would be two options: to part company or not to part company. Parting company could mean parting for good or until meeting again on a friendly or more-than-friendly basis.

'Phew...I think I'm done.' Celia placed the napkin on the table and tapped her stomach.

Ardcock reached into his wallet to begin preparations for paying his half of the bill plus fifty per-cent of the tip. She thanked him, which, in a way, was odd. Taking all things into consideration it should be him thanking her.

On leaving the restaurant Ardcock looked in both directions. Celia remarked that she could do with a drink to help the food go down. The observation was either a point of information or an invitation to join her. Going for a drink after eating Indian food and viewing an art-exhibition seemed logical enough.

'How about you?' He pulled his coat tighter and checked with his watch. Just after seven-o-clock in the evening wasn't a bad time to be going for a drink.

'Well...' she said, looking him in the eye. 'Let me buy you a drink.'

'No,' he said, reflecting on events so far: tangerines picked off the floor of the greengrocers, coffee, ice-cream, the entrance fee to an art-exhibition and the drinks in a restaurant – there came a point when enough was enough.

'Enough is enough.' Which wasn't saying he couldn't use a drink, just that *he* should buy *her* a drink. 'Let me buy you a drink.'

Celia wasn't inclined to argue. 'Go on then...I'll let you. Where do you fancy?'

To the best of Ardcock's knowledge there were two pubs in the vicinity, both within walking distance: *The Flying*

Dutchman and *The Fox In A Box*. Both roughly the same distance though *The Flying Dutchman* was a few hundred yards closer and probably wasn't as busy. Which were two reasons for suggesting it.

'Fine,' she said. '*The Flying Dutchman* it is.'

At the pub he ordered a pint of lager. Celia asked for half a cider. She took her seat whilst he bought the drinks. He'd ordered lager on the grounds it was a safer option. With beer you never knew what to expect: it could be good or bad depending on circumstances beyond your control. .

'So – you're a lager-man,' Celia remarked as he took his seat opposite. He told her it was a safer option.

Ardcock looked at his glass, eyeing a scum of bubbles as he tilted it to the light.

'Okay?' she asked. He said 'yes'.

Conversations in pubs tend to have the edge on conversations elsewhere. Celia being the sociable type but not excessively so, suited Ardcock, who – in the case of the latter – was similarly inclined. Which wasn't to say they'd sit in total silence.

She asked about work and he told her a bit about it, but not a huge amount as he didn't have a lot to say when it came to talking about work. She told him she was an assistant in a school which meant helping children who needed help. Ardcock was of the opinion most children needed help but opted not to say anything to the effect as it might come across as being sarcastic or flippant – neither of which he had any inclination to be.

Following the pub there were two possibilities: go their separate ways, or stay together. Staying together at this stage of proceedings and at this time of night could be an indication of something more serious in the air, which – itself – had certain implications.

'Well...' Celia had stretched back in her seat and yawned. She seemed to be implying it might be time to go. Ardcock had a third of his drink left. He drank it in one go and put the glass back on the table.

Outside the stars were out and Ardcock noticed the wind had gained in strength.

On stepping onto the pavement Celia pulled her coat tighter and eyed the full length of the street. 'I always find this time of day a little strange if I'm away from the flat – neither early nor late – neither one thing nor the other.' Ardcock could see her point.

Which – stood on the step of the pub with night approaching – could prove to be significant.

'Well, if you'd like coffee, the invitation's there.' Ardcock noticed how she made a point of looking towards the sea-front.

'Where?' he asked, feeling he ought to put the question whether or not it was entirely necessary.

'Why not back at my place?' she said, turning to address him directly.

It was a simple question phrased as was often the case – as a negative…why *not* her place? There was no obvious reason not to drink coffee at her place as the most obvious other places – cafes – would be shut. Hence his response…

'Why not?'

They walked side by side but with a bit of a gap between them. She said she liked to walk through the town at night when it was quiet and you had time to think. He agreed it was sometimes a good idea to do that though he didn't go into reasons. She asked how he was fixed to walk rather than getting a cab. 'Walk off some of that curry.' She tapped her stomach. Ardcock saw no reason not to walk rather than spend money on a cab.

'Okay,' she said, indicating the direction once they got to the first turning. 'That settles that.'

The walk to her flat took approximately twenty-three minutes. They talked about the advantages of walking as opposed to relying on public transport that at this time of night you could never rely on. Having similar views on the issue the conversation switched to their futures, Celia being reasonably settled where she was living but given to bouts of restlessness, which meant often being on the lookout for something new, Ardcock's inclination being to stick to what he knew, depending on circumstances.

On arriving at her flat she led the way in. It was a comfortable two bedroom flat, handy for the shops and a bus stop only a few yards away.

Offering positive comments when you first enter someone's home can be a positive move: acknowledging a major feature of their life like a change of jobs or getting married or dying.

He told her it was a decent place. She said it suited her needs, directing his eye to a share of a small garden at the rear of the property and indoor storage space in the cubby-hole at the end of the hall. Ardcock commented that a cubby-hole to put things in was a useful feature. In some flats you didn't get that.

The coffee arrived – an not-unexpected development in the context of the day as a whole.

'Mints?' A dish of mints was placed on the table. Mints freshened your breath and aided digestion, a consideration after eating spicy food. Ardcock reached for a mint.

With mints consumed Celia turned to the cupboard and produced a bottle of brandy she'd had sitting on the shelf for ages waiting for that 'special moment'. Ardcock watched the bottle being planted firmly in the centre of the table, all indications being this could be deemed to be a 'special moment' – something of an event, confirming that a relationship, of sorts, had clearly been established, the circumstances of which would depend on a number of factors. Ardcock wasn't inclined to rule anything out any more than he was inclined to rule anything in.

Celia had left the top off the brandy bottle and ten minutes later she tilted the bottle above Ardcock's glass, adding a generous measure to the few drops sitting in the glass. Celia raised her glass. Ardcock raised his glass.

Minutes later she suggested moving to the lounge. Ardcock could see the advantage in sitting in what would be more comfortable surroundings though he still had his bag of shopping. The issue was whether to leave it in the kitchen or take it to the lounge. Taking a bag of shopping into someone's lounge would be a strange move so he made a decision to leave it in the kitchen.

There was an armchair and a sofa in the lounge. Plus – a tv and a hi-fi sound system. The question was where Ardcock would sit. The armchair was a possibility. Sitting on the sofa was another possibility but depended on where Celia intended to sit.

She had seated herself on the sofa and was tapping the space next to her. Clearly her intention was that Ardcock should join her on the sofa. Not doing so would seem impolite after drinking coffee and brandy. Plus – the sofa was more comfortable than the chair.

She watched him sink into the cushion of the sofa, observing features that had barely changed since they'd first met in the greengrocers – much like his manner – odd but strangely endearing. 'Unassuming' was a way of putting it. She could think of less attractive features in the case of many men.

The drinks were beginning to take effect. She drank her brandy and replenished Ardcock's glass.

'Well,' she said, putting the bottle back on the table and sinking into her seat. 'Here we are.'

So there they were – somewhere close to midnight seated on a sofa drinking brandy after drinks in a pub, an Indian meal and a visit to an art exhibition – all following coffee and ice-cream in a café after picking a few tangerines off the floor of the greengrocers. Celia sighed as Ardcock manoeuvred the cushion to aid his posture.

'All right?' Celia was watching him.

Ardcock nodded. It was good brandy, or he supposed it was good brandy. He wasn't exactly sure of the difference between 'good' and 'bad' brandy, except to some people it was an issue, as was whisky.

A development during the next few minutes was Celia leaning towards Ardcock's shoulder – the indication being she might soon be leaning *on* his shoulder.

Which, moments later, proved to be the case – she *did* lean on his shoulder, as in… lean her *head* on his shoulder.

'Do you mind?'

Seated on a sofa, brandy in one hand, Celia reclining on his shoulder – there was little to object to. He told her so and was instantly rewarded with a topping-up of his glass.

Later – fully relaxed and possibly beginning to feel the effects of the brandy on top of the drinks in the pub, she told Ardcock he was a 'funny one'. Arguably a fitting enough comment to level at someone disinclined to be anything other than his own man.

'I think so,' she said, taking a lack of response as invitation to repeat the point and snuggle closer.

Moments later she wriggled so as to manoeuvre her head against his shoulder. Ardcock took another drink. Celia sighed and reached for her glass.

Given the circumstances a number of possibilities sprang to mind. One of which was to stick around and see how things transpired. The question was whether there was a reason *not* to stick around and see how things transpired? Not as far as he could see. He took another drink and sank back in the cushion.

They talked of their sleeping habits which were similar though not identical. They touched on other topics, like sport. Celia pressed him on it. Ardcock had no strong feelings on the subject. The fact that some people – or horses – ran quicker than others or jumped higher – or were more dextrous at controlling a ball; or that if you put two men in a ring and asked them to hit each other, one might get the upper hand and/or eventually knock the other out – came as no surprise to him.

She looked him in the eye.

'What about other things?' She was staring, her voice as still as his expression. 'Do you ever think about other things, you know – things that go on in the world?'

Ardcock considered the question, aware that answers to such questions required a little thought. People, he knew, tended to have views about things, particularly things that went on in the world – things they frequently had only scant knowledge of which made it less a point-of-view than feeling a need to say something, a trait that should come as a surprise to no-one – certainly not to Ardcock. But she'd put the question and it deserved an answer.

'Yes and no,' he said.

Celia nodded.

'I sometimes think about things when I take long walks along the sea-front, especially when it's breezy.' Ardcock took another drink of brandy and leant back into the cushion, where, a few minutes later, an arm reached across to come to rest a few inches above his left hip. She turned to face him.

'Do you mind?'

Ardcock had no reason to object – in acknowledgement of which he placed an arm over the rear of the sofa.

When Celia next spoke it was accompanied by a sigh and a hand tightening just below his rib-cage. She told him he mustn't get the wrong idea. That she didn't make a habit of inviting men back to her flat late at night to drink brandy.

To Ardcock such things were neither here nor there. As far as he could make out she was disposed to being her own woman – in respect of which she had little call to justify herself.

For a while silence took over: a silence that – after a while – warranted interruption.

Putting her glass to one side and turning her face towards him, she stretched to plant a kiss on the side of Ardcock's right cheek.

It was a firm kiss, the kind where the lips lingered longer than the kind of kiss when you met a relative. And it had been accompanied by a light brushing of her right breast against him which might or might not have been intentional. It was difficult to be sure of such things without asking. Ardcock wasn't inclined to ask. But – it called for a response...

Putting his glass on the table he turned to face her. Seconds later, their lips met. And seconds after that, having kissed her warmly on the lips, their lips parted but only with his hand placed lightly on the area beneath her right shoulder.

She mumbled something Ardcock failed to hear but surmised might not be of huge importance. When they next kissed Ardcock parted his lips, extending his tongue to brush against her tongue protruding slightly above her lower lip. She appeared to approve and positioned herself to accept the gesture, partaking in a third kiss along the lines of the second but with a further parting of the lips. Plus – intentionally more than unintentionally – Ardcock's hand finding its way onto her right breast, where – meeting little resistance – it remained for something like fifteen to twenty seconds.

Which, given the circumstances – close to midnight following beer, brandy, a meal in an Indian restaurant, coffee, ice-cream and a visit to an art exhibition – would likely come as a surprise to no-one. Certainly not to Ardcock who, in any respect, was hardly one to be dictated to by the hands on a watch.

There are occasions when 'going to bed' doesn't mean going to bed in the literal sense of the phrase. All things considered, 'going to bed' with Celia had been a distinct possibility for something like an hour to an hour and a half or even longer.

When it happened it was hardly unexpected. Ardcock, who was directly involved in the decision, had asked himself whether there was a reason *not* to go to bed with her? Not as far as he could see. Particularly given he had made it his business to be an astute student/observer of the art – or science – of 'making love'. The success of which appeared to be down to such factors as the time of day, the setting, the extent of the participants' arousal and particularly the mood the woman was in. The bed was an ideal setting, as was the time of day. And Celia's mood was that of a woman wishing to be made love to. Or at least so it appeared to Ardcock, whose arousal – on having fondled each other intimately for something like fifteen minutes – was close to completion.

All indications were that with a touch of inspiration, imagination and a little forward planning – they'd be disposed to 'making love' to something close to maximum effect.

Which – to all intents and purposes – proved to be the case. By Ardcock's watch (though far from one to have such occasions governed by the hands on a watch) it was ten minutes into the stage commonly referred to as 'foreplay' that – with Celia opting for the customary 'missionary position' – Ardcock positioned himself above her in order to engage in the act of 'making love' to her.

'You're quite a one Ardcock,' Celia had said, uttering his name repeatedly, adopting her own rhythmic approach to coincide with Ardcock's synchronised thrusting of the hips. There'd be no argument from Ardcock.

Only on completion of the act – moaning and sweating slightly and turning on her side to scrape a finger-nail along the length of his shoulder-blade, did her head come to rest on his chest, the pair's co-ordinated sense of timing enabling them to take a breather whilst witnessing the clock's ticks bidding their way to the onset of a new day – ticks every bit as resonant as the beat of Ardcock's heart.

'Mmm...' She shuffled closer. 'I can hear your heart beating...tic toc, tic toc...like a robot...'

She looked up, reflecting on what – all things considered – had turned out to be a quite unexpected turn of events, sighing and squeezing Ardcock's midriff with both arms pulled tight around him. 'But you're not a robot are you?' She flexed both arms, speaking through tightly drawn lips. 'You're Ardcock.'

She was right. It *had* been quite a day. And speaking as a man lying next to a woman he had just made love to, after consuming ice-cream, coffee, Indian food, beer and brandy, following a chance encounter in a greengrocers – he was hardly inclined to dispute the fact. He was – after all – his own man; always had been and always would be.

* * * * *

End Of Course Assignment

R. T. Entwistle BA. (Hons) MA.(Cantab) put his case to one side and took a mug from the counter.

'Had an interesting one today.' He swirled a mug with *If you can't teach...lecture!* emblazoned across it under the tap a few times and reached for a pot of coffee.

'Dick Winters – final year student in this morning's seminar. I'd given them the date for submitting the title of their Final Assignment. I don't know if you know him – skinny chap with fuzzy hair, walks with a limp. Anyway – it was the usual procedure, each taking their turn to give us their title and add a few details, and when it got to his turn he just looked round each member of the group and just came out with it – said he intended to write something of his own!'

Tebbit looked up.

'Write something of his own? Like what?'

Entwistle shrugged, the contents of the cup allowed a moment to settle before moving to join his colleague wrestling with a pile of papers.

'You mean 'write' as in...*write* ?'

'Presumably.'

'Write what exactly?'

There was a moment's hesitation.

'I believe he said something along the lines of...*writing a short story!*'

'Short story?'

Eyebrows were raised...a pile of green tagged manuscript papers temporarily put to one side to consider the implications of what he was hearing.

'How bizarre.' He turned, allowing his colleague time to settle, his observation as much one of puzzlement as surprise. 'What I don't understand is why anyone would think such an idea is remotely relevant. I mean – we take them through the whole cannon – from *Medieval, Celtic, The Classics, The Romantics,* the *Post-Modernism of the 50's, 60's...*and this chap turns up on the doorstep and tells us he wants to...*write something of his own!*'

Entwistle conceded the point, taking his seat whilst attempting to avoid spilling the contents of the mug onto freshly pressed trousers.

'I know, it's hard to imagine what goes on in some of their minds.'

Tebbit sighed, taking a moment to shed some light on the dizzy mind-sets of some of their students.

'What about the others. Any other bizarre ideas about to be dumped in our sad, not to say...unsuspecting laps?'

Settling himself, Entwistle set about recalling a handful of titles likely to be heading their way over the coming weeks: *Hemmingway's place in the post-war American psyche... Orwell as 'misguided misanthropist'* and one of the female students taking a critical look at *the mores and conventions of post thirties American feminism'...*

Tebbit nodded agreeably.

'Well – at least some strains of sanity prevail.'

For a moment silence prevailed – broken only by a hand reaching to rest lightly on his colleague's arm.

'Still, I suppose it could have been worse. At least the chap didn't come up with any half-baked ideas about writing his own poetry!'

There was jollity on both sides of the chair arm, Entwistle reaching for his coffee, Tebbit back to thumbing his way through *Observations Of The Early Augustan Verse* awaiting attention in his lap.

Only after some delay did the grip tighten on his friend's arm.

'By the way – you really must find the time to pop along to the Art Department to cast an eye on some of their students' Final Assignments. Some wonderful paintings – quite outstanding.'

Having finished what remained of his coffee, he was back to rinsing the vessel under the nearest tap, an eye raised in appreciation.

'The imagination those chaps bring to their work – quite staggering,' he said.

* * * * *

'Okay...'

Dave Jessop, a teacher of some twenty nine years standing, perches himself on a desk, his preferred position for observing developments through a measured, calculating eye – a technique he has no intention of abandoning in order to start bellowing and issuing threats, neither of which would be practical or prove beneficial in establishing the atmosphere for learning – as in *real* 'learning' – to take place.

Some fall into line. After a minute or so he's got about a fifth of the class in-tow. Maria Davis, Thelma Walker and Alison Michaels are attentive. As are four more sitting next to the aisles. It's often the girls who are first to settle, which isn't being sexist because in this class it's a fact. But not all are girls. Two boys are also ready and waiting for the lesson to begin.

Jade Samuel is also quiet – rocking back and forth on her seat to the sounds emanating from an earpiece inserted and held in place in one ear. She issues threats to Thomas Pathe who makes an attempt to grab the phone, scraping his chair noisily along the floor in the process, whilst in an opposite corner of the room – Wayne Oxborrow and Matthew Tolley's teasing graduates to a play-fight, encouraged by those occupying the neighbouring seats, two of which take a tumble when a spat-out lump of chewing gum lands in Hilary Nonce's hair: a full-scale attack on the perpetrator following close at hand.

Unabashed and likely undisturbed by developments in her vicinity, Susan Mellor reproaches one of the boys who has swiped the pencil-case from under her nose and now waves it in the air upside down, spilling pens, pencils, coloured pencils, rubbers, shavings and other assorted debris on the floor where a forest of hands reach to claim ownership of whichever contents are set to head fortuitously in their direction.

Whilst a few desks away the play-fights continue to gather momentum: Bradley Harcourt quick to seek revenge for a paper aeroplane nose-diving into his ear launches himself at Ronnie Mc.Farlane who laughs, aiming a wayward punch.

All of which proves too much for Carol Smith's chair. Unable or unwilling to accommodate her balanced at such a precarious angle any longer – it sends her toppling to the floor midst hoots of derision, as – a few seats to the front – Jonathan Mellor swears at Aaron Tilby using the f word, Susan Mellor throws punches at the boy who took her pencil case and the girl with chewing-gum in her hair begins a spirited circuit of the room in pursuit of Marcus Hanks.

A pursuit soon to be seen gathering pace: Damian Price, Timothy Bones, Bradley Harcourt and Ronnie Mc.Farlane – all eager to be seen joining in the fray, completing several circuits of the room, ending up at the door, exiting the door and heading off – one imagines – into the great beyond.

Meanwhile back at the chalk-face – Jonathan Baker (whose mother is a dog) swears at Susan Mellor (whose mother is both a prostitute and a dog.)

Whilst a few seats away, Jade Samuel's pursuit of Thomas Pathe leads to a firm kick in the balls. 'A hit, a very palpable hit' comes the cry as the boy (whose mother is a dog, a prostitute – and a lesbian) follows Jade Samuel (who, along with her mother, is a dog, a lesbian – and a tramp) to the door, through the door and off – one imagines – into the great beyond.

It is on witnessing a good two-thirds of the class having fled the nest that an uneasy calm descends, a handful of malingerers exchanging looks that bear the hallmarks of a temporary truce – that perhaps, for now, enough is enough.

The moment for Jessop to signal to Maria Davis who – without hint of a reaction – lifts a set of texts from a nearby shelf, a third of which are distributed to the adjacent desks.

The signal for Thelma Walker to cast a nod at Jonathan Woodley – the pair noting that…on the 7th February at approximately twelve minutes and fifty seconds into Lesson 3 – 'learning' as in…*real* learning…could finally take place!

In an atmosphere as calm as a millpond – Jessop turns to view what remains of his class through a measured and calculating eye.

'Okay,' he says… 'Let's get started…'

* * * * *

Note: Around 2013 – 15 (and possibly beyond) a number of tv programmes, some bearing titles prefixed '*Educating____here there – and just about everywhere*'…laid claim – at least in part – to be depicting life in 'difficult' classrooms! The events described above are closer to life in a 'difficult' classroom than such programmes come anywhere near depicting.

[plus…an invitation to spare a thought for thousands of pupils whose school experience is savaged on a daily basis by the 'challenging behaviours' of a significant number of their fellow pupils.]

A (Blind) Man And His Dog

[True story]

The man making his way down the right hand side of the railway overpass was blind. The shuffling walk, the dark glasses, the long white stick and a Golden Labrador dog strutting alongside in its bright fluorescent jacket and tethered to a harness clutched firmly in the man's grasp – all evidence to the fact.

The elderly woman approaching from the opposite direction deduced as much, easing herself to one side to give man and dog sufficient space to pass.

It was as their paths came close to crossing that the man – sensing someone's presence, stopped – his unseeing eye searching in the direction of the footsteps. The dog, aware some interruption was imminent, stopped with him, waiting patiently at his side for the interruption to pass.

'Excuse me,' he said, making every effort to speak clearly to help convince whoever it was to grant him a minute or two of their time.

The woman stopped to look into the face of the man, wondering what someone in his position – ie. a blind man – could possibly be wanting with the likes of her.

'I'm sorry to bother you but could you tell me the best – or the *quickest* way to get to Sainsburys please?' The man knew he was basically on the right track but wasn't sure exactly which turning to take once on the road at the end of the path.

The woman thought for a moment, relieved she wasn't being asked to donate money or deal with some issue involving the dog.

Figuring what she believed to be the best route to take, she stopped to consider how best to communicate it.

Leaning from the waist and clearing her throat to help ensure she would be understood – she informed the dog that, as far as she knew, the best bet was to take a left at the end of the path and then a right turn which would bring them onto a road where another right turn would lead them to the shop a few hundred yards on the right hand side. Continuing to stare for confirmation it had registered – the dog, sensing it was the focus of some attention, yet trained to guard against unwanted and unwarranted consequences of such attention, peered back, and then at his owner for confirmation all was in order.

It was as she was in the process of straightening herself, awarding herself a pat on the back for having done her good deed for the day, that a voice thanked her – suggesting a path that cut through the first row of houses might save them a few more minutes.

Staring hard at the dog, the woman turned to address the man.

'I have to say...' she said, pointing at the dog. 'That's a remarkably clever dog you've got there. I'd no idea there was a short-cut between the houses...Well done dog...Well done indeed!'

It was with a final glance at both man and dog that the woman continued on her way, assured that the maxim 'we learn something new every day' was still alive and kicking.

A few yards behind man and dog exchanged glances – relieved that they too would shortly be on *their* way to the shop that both guessed was something like a ten minute walk depending on whether they'd take the short-cut through the houses.

* * * * *

[Based on an incident featured on BBC radio in October '15 when – during a Radio 5 phone-in asking blind people for their experiences – a man told how on asking a woman passing by for directions to get to a shop, the woman leant to issue her instructions to the man's seeing-eye dog!]

Our Charlotte

The scene is a Comprehensive School's 'Meet The Teacher' evening. The setting – the school hall with desks arranged round its perimeter. Three chairs are assigned to each desk: one on one side and two facing. Malcolm Dicktopper – one of a handful of English teachers on duty seated behind a semi-cluttered desk – consults a list and looks up. On catching his eye two parents abandon their seat in the central aisle and approach his desk. Dicktopper has made a decision this time round to shake all their hands. He's noticed most teachers – particularly the younger teachers – make a point of shaking every parent's hand, which on thinking about it, doesn't seem like a bad idea: fending off accusations of being standoffish, making them feel like their attendance is appreciated, which – in some cases – it is.

Setting eyes on the parents for the first time is often an education in itself; some barely out of their teens from the look of it; how every year they looked younger: dads' tattoos rapidly running out of space alongside rings protruding from places you'd never imagined they'd fit.

Mum seems anxious about announcing the name to anyone within earshot other than her husband who's about to take the seat next to her: a seat that with luck will grant him a decent view of the Girls' PE teacher seated two desks away.

She leans forward, hoping to set the tone for what's likely to follow, a glint of optimism saddled with one of trepidation – a feeling shared both sides of the desk….

'Charlotte Mason. How's she doing?

Dicktopper sifts through a pile of paper on a desk too small to contain it.

'Pretty good.' A finger scrolls a hastily convened barrage of statistics...*past-levels...current-levels...target-levels, short-term targets, long-term targets, value-added*...notions significantly less quantifiable than your average politician has the wherewithal – or inclination – to grasp.

'Oh good.' She curls her fingers into a ball and looks to her left.

'She likes English, don't she Trev?'

Trev nods. It's designed to sweeten him a little. If they like the subject they might get nicer things said about them.

'Loves reading.' Mum wriggles in her seat. 'I goes to her of a night...'Charlotte darlin' get to sleep; the book'll still be there in the morning."

It is whilst on the subject of books that mum thinks it's best to put him in the picture, her voice lowering to keep it strictly between the two of them.

'The thing is Mr. Dicktopper, we think she might be *dyslexic.*'

She sits back, relieved to have finally got it off her chest and waiting to see what reaction it gets.

'We had her tested at juniors. But they didn't seem to spot it – did they Trev?'

'Din't do nothing at juniors,' Trev says.

Dicktopper taps his pen. It's a tricky issue for teachers, particularly English teachers – not least in attempting to grasp exactly what it means, aside from a tendency to get the letters in words confused. Ninety per-cent of kids in schools get the letters in some words confused. And – it being a convenient hook on which to hang a whole host of shortcomings. The best bet in such situations – an undertaking to look into it with the appropriate member of staff and to keep an eye out for significant developments.

Dicktopper scribbles a note. Another useful ploy – be seen scribbling a note on whatever slip of paper happens to be at hand.

Mrs. Mason watches and leans into the desk.

'It's a shame because she loves writing stories. Don't she Trev? Trev nods.

'And it ain't easy writing stories if you're *dyslexic*.' She looks across at her husband. 'You was *dyslexic* when you was at school, weren't you Trev?'

'Something like that. Din't call it that then; just said you was thick. Weren't no good at writing stories though.'

He feels for his pouch of Golden Virginia wondering if he'll get away with sloping off for a quick smoke before the next appointment.

With the *dyslexia* issue temporarily sorted, Mrs. Mason turns again on Dicktopper.

'Now while we're on the subject Mr. Dicktopper.' She has both hands placed firmly on the desk. 'What I want to know is...do you teach them *spelling*?'

For once Dicktopper appears to be ready with his answer.

'We certainly do Mrs. Mason.'

'Cos we think spelling's important, don't we Trev? Trev nods.

'But the thing is about Juniors, they didn't do nothing about their spelling did they Trev?

Trev shakes his head.

'Din't give a shit.'

I say to her when she'd doin' her homework. 'Have you checked your spelling? She goes 'yes'. And when I check, I can't tell whether she has or she hasn't 'cause my spelling's terrible. And yours ain't no better is it Trev? 'cause you was dyslexic.' Trev shakes his head.

Dicktopper taps the pen and looks Mrs. Mason in the eye.

'We definitely keep an eye on their spelling.'

'But do you *teach* them?'

He thinks of his most expedient answer. If he says 'yes' then he might have to explain *what* they teach them. Which is difficult in so far as he's not quite sure what, if anything, they *do* actually teach them. But he can't say 'no'.

He draws closer to the desk.

'We find the most effective way to deal with spelling is to address it as and when it crops up in their work.' He watches her scribble something on her appointment slip. Spelling is one of Mrs. Mason's hobbyhorses. When she spots a misspelling in a sign outside a shop she's likely to go bursting right in there and tell them – to their face.

Moments later she's back to her notes, fingering her way down the page and stopping at a point close to the bottom.

'And do you give them homework?'

'Oh yes. They get homework on a regular basis – at least from *me*,' he adds, quick to disassociate himself from less responsible colleagues who systematically fail to set the pupils homework.

"Cause we think homework's important, don't we Trev?' Trev nods.

"Cause she don't seem to get much homework at all. We say Charlotte 'Homework first...Facebook second.' But she says 'we ain't got no homework' and goes straight on Facebook.'

She shuffles in her seat, recollections of being bombarded with homework when she was at school more evident than the likelihood of her ever getting round to doing any of it.

'Thing is Mr. Dicktopper, they never used to give them any homework at Juniors, did they Trev?'

'Din't do nothin' at Juniors. Din't teach 'em nothing.'

'Now...' She does another quick check with her list, a finger halting at what promises to be another bone of contention. She leans to look Dicktopper in the eye.

'Do you teach them *grammar*?'

Dicktopper thinks. Another tricky one; aside from a need to sound reasonably convincing.

'We certainly do Mrs. Mason.' He hopes the assurance will fend off enquiries as to *what* they actually teach them.

'Good. 'Cause we think grammar's important. And at Juniors they didn't teach them no grammar did they Trev?' Trev shakes his head.

Mrs, Mason, appeased for the present, watches him and strikes another tick on her sheet, fingering her way through a further column of statistics. She stops to examine the ones at the top of her list as Tracy Unwin, a girl in Dicktopper's tutor-group, approaches on tea-duty, offering him a cup – or one of those flimsy plastic beakers that severely indent at the slightest touch. He takes the cup attempting to place in on a free spot on the desk without slopping its contents over his records and Mrs. Mason's documentation. She allows him time for a much-earned drink. It's likely thirsty work being a teacher on evenings like this.

The reprieve is temporary.

'The thing is Mr. Dicktopper. We've been following Charlotte's *Levels*.

Dicktopper positions himself to view the document she was handed on arrival more effectively.

Mrs. Mason extends the relevant page for mutual appraisal.

'It says Charlotte can...*sustain ideas*...and *develop them in interesting ways*. Which we're pleased about.' She looks again, following the line onto the description beneath. 'It says what she's got to do is...*convey meaning in a range of forms* and *identify layers of meaning...*'

She stops to give it a second look, checking she's got it right.

'The thing is Mr. Dicktopper ...do you teach them *meaning in a range of forms* and *identifying layers of meaning?*'

Dicktopper nods.

'We certainly do Mrs. Mason. Pretty much on a day to day basis in fact.'

'Good.' Mrs. Mason strikes a tick and thumbs down the page. 'Cause we think that's important, don't we Trev?' Trev nods.

'Cause they din't teach them nothing about that at Juniors, did they Trev. Trev shakes his head. 'Din't teach them nothing.'

'Okay Mr. Dicktopper – now.' She shuffles into position for what's likely to be the final throw of the dice.

'What we want to know is…is there anything *we* can do to help?'

Dicktopper leans to meet her eyeball to eyeball.

'Encourage her to read Mrs. Mason; any sort of reading, any opportunity she gets.' He watches her scribble on what limited space remains on the sheet.

'The importance of reading can't be overstated,' he says, eager to take full advantage of the least controversial advice she'll be receiving all evening.

Mrs. Mason's back to her sheet, a finger working its way to the end of a line.

'Okay Mr. Dicktopper.' She checks with her list. '*Spelling… Grammar…Levels* – that's English done!' She strikes a bold tick in the relevant box.

'Now what's next…?' She shuffles the papers, getting them into some semblance of order and consults with the appointment sheet. 'PE.'

Trev looks up, resolved to having the baccy pouch stay put a while longer.

'Well thankyou Mr. Dicktopper.'

'Thankyou Mrs. Mason.' He makes a point of shaking both their hands as two more parents vacate their seats in the central aisle to make their way towards him. They take their seats. Dicktopper extends a hand.

'Carol Wainthorpe's parents.' Mum leans forwards, the appointment sheet placed on the desk before them.

'How's she doing?'

'Pretty good,' Dicktopper says.

'Oh good..But___' Mrs. Wainthorpe leans to look in his direction.

'We're worried about her spelling.' She leans closer….

* * * * *

Weight Matters

Positioning myself for the closing shots – lying on my back, bum raised slightly off the bed, eyes fixed directly on the camera with both my – what Tanya playfully referred to as... zeppelin-like boobs – cupped and raised from my chest – I had the feeling I was beginning to get the hang of it.

'Good darling.' It seemed to be one of Tanya's stock phrases, stepping this way and that, snapping away waiting for her assistant, Hilary, to hand her various gadgets from a metal box. 'You look good Monica.' I didn't say anything back because it wasn't the kind of comment that warranted a response. I didn't know whether I was 'looking good'. I know I was feeling incredibly hot under the lights and finding it hard not to keep squinting, but beyond that I didn't feel I was in a position to comment.

Looking back on how it all began: the two women from downstairs knocking on my door at nine-o-clock on a Monday evening had been a strange enough development in itself. The house is one of those big rambling suburban houses spread over three floors. Six flats in all. The point being none of us know that much about each other, or care that much, truth be told.

Which made the appearance of the women who lived in one of the ground-floor flats something of a mystery. I'd seen them around and gathered that the one with the short black pixie-style hair – the more up-front one – was a photographer; the other one I wasn't sure about other than they seemed to operate very much as a pair. I was a bit puzzled. People turning up on your doorstep was unusual at any time. When I saw them standing there I assumed it was some problem or a complaint; something to do with putting the rubbish out or too much noise, not that I make any noise you could hear elsewhere. Which was maybe why I invited them in. Presumably it was something that mattered or they wouldn't have been knocking on my door at that hour.

I offered them a coffee but they said no. On taking a seat they looked at each other once or twice and immediately started talking, though it was Tanya – the more outgoing one – who did the talking, telling me about her line of work; that she was a photographer and on seeing me around had come up with an idea and had a proposition to put to me. For a moment that was it, like I already needed time to consider what she was saying. I couldn't imagine what it would be.

She quickly set about putting me in the picture, telling me she'd recently switched to an area of photography that – as she put it – was to do with the 'female-form' presented in what might be described as a variety-of-guises, deliberately being very matter-of-fact about it, coming out with phrases to make it sound nothing out of the ordinary, though to me not always making sense. Pointing out how fashions come and go and how people's photographic tastes can vary almost from one day to the next. I still wasn't sure why she was telling me all this but I guessed she had a reason so I listened as she went on to say that people working in their field ie. 'people' photographers – were always on the lookout for something different; that the stick-thin models everyone expects to see in magazines or draped over car bonnets in advertisements were a bit old-hat. Which I kind of understood but still not entirely. Stopping a moment and sensing a need to tread carefully – ie. choose her words carefully – what she was saying was the 'anorexic-look' was out. What was now 'in' and very much the trend in current photography, was something a little different. Again – she made a point of stopping to emphasise the point. Different, but essentially, no different! That representations of the human form – in all its guises – was ultimately one and the same.

Though I was listening I still couldn't quite make out what she meant or what it had to do with me. Which was probably what prompted her to come straight out with it and make her point: without wishing to be unkind or in any way unsympathetic to people in my position (again this was her way of putting it) pointing out that my weight could be about to do me a huge favour. She stopped as if having come out with such a bold statement I'd likely need time to think about what she was saying – even though I still had only a vague idea as to where it was all leading.

I'd never fooled myself when it came to my appearance. The fact is: I'm fat – or 'severely overweight' as some people choose to put it. And possibly as a consequence I'd never regarded myself as 'pretty' or in any way magazine material, not that these things have ever mattered to me or are in any way important. It isn't easy to see yourself as 'pretty' when you're close to sixteen stones because your face gets overlooked due to everything around it. Or so I'd imagined...

The way Tanya put it; again she was thinking carefully about how best to phrase it – my face was a 'warm' face, which I thought was pushing it a bit, but in her view was a huge plus!

Which was when she went on to explain what she had in mind: to take photographs of me in a variety of poses, again stopping so as not to give the wrong impression – that in in no way were they coming at it from a sexual or pornographic angle; that they were in the business of celebrating the human form rather than exploiting it..

She went on to explain that their flat was, in effect, a mini studio. The idea being to take a number of shots of me posing in front of the camera, shots she could guarantee would draw the attention of at least a handful of magazines. And, she didn't hesitate to add – would lead to a cheque for two hundred pounds passing hands at the conclusion of the first 'shoot', a kind of down-payment – confirmation there was money to be made at both ends of the chain, so to speak.

When they'd gone I made a cup of tea and put the television on to think about what they'd said, particularly the bit about the 'girl-next-door' look that I wasn't entirely sure about. The idea of my disability [which is the word that sometimes gets used] being viewed in a similar light to photographs of slim or 'ordinary' women just didn't ring true – the kind of thing they'd maybe want me to hear. But for reasons that were still far from clear.

It was only on thinking about it later that it occurred I might be jumping to conclusions a little too quickly which had always been a tendency of mine; to act first and think later, letting my heart rule my head was the way my mother would put it. I wasn't a photographer. It's easy to dismiss ideas simply because it isn't what you expect to hear. And you don't have to be an expert to know that 'art', 'photography' – whichever word suits – *does* tend to come in all shapes and sizes; that people's tastes in these things do change: that the women in old-fashioned paintings were nearly always big rather than slim. And when it comes to art and photography, things that might seem....let's not say *ugly* but *unusual*...can attract the eye just as much as what people expect to see, maybe for that very reason. And if Tanya was right, that, for once, my weight was in a position to do me a favour – why dismiss it out of hand? Not least, given the fact that they'd taken time and trouble to come and talk to me about it.

It was the following day that I knocked on their door to tell them I'd given it some thought and decided I'd give it a go but with the understanding that if it didn't work out or if I wasn't happy with it then I would stop. They – or rather Tanya agreed instantly, saying it was one of the biggest and most important decision of my life and she was sure I wouldn't regret it. I couldn't be sure about that but there are times when you need to take a chance, and maybe this was my time. And I'm not going to pretend the money wasn't an issue. I didn't earn much working at the supermarket and was sometimes scrimping and scraping to get by. It would be nice to have some money to buy some nice clothes and go on holiday and maybe move into a nice flat. And at some point maybe buy a little flat of my own!

All of which was fine in theory but still seemed a million miles away when I plucked up the courage to knock on their door a few days later for the first 'shoot' as Tanya called it.

The instructions I'd been given were to shower and use a certain shampoo and dry my hair in a certain way – confirmation that what I was getting into wasn't just a few quick snap-shots in front of a camera. Brought home even more by their insistence on me wearing make-up. So far Tanya had said nothing about using make-up and I asked if it was really necessary. I don't care much for make-up and never wore it. She assured me it was pretty essential but promised to go easy with it. It involved a bit of blush and eye-liner and something I can't remember the name of, which I suppose wasn't too bad, and as they pointed out, I'd soon get used to it. When I say 'they' it was still Tanya doing all the talking, Hilary busy getting stuff ready for the cameras and the tripod.

It felt odd – a bit like undressing in the middle of a busy shop to try on some new clothes instead of in the changing-room – standing in front of the two women wearing a turquoise gown, make-up and no bra, being urged to lie on the bed and make myself comfortable whilst they made a few adjustments to the camera.

The idea was to stretch out on the duvet with the gown half unfolded across me, without a bra and wearing knickers that were dark green – looking constantly at the camera with my eyes wide and one leg slightly folded. From then on it was a question of removing the smock bit by bit which was embarrassing at first but the way they, or mainly Tanya, put it helped. Reminding me that they – ie. 'we' – were simply en couraging people to view others in a way they weren't accustomed to seeing them.

From then on it wasn't too embarrassing except when she asked me to 'cup my boobs'...taking both breasts (which are pretty big) in my palms and kind of weigh them up and down. Tanya seemed okay with the way I was doing it. Again it took a bit of getting used to but once you've done it for a few minutes it's not so bad. It just felt a bit strange because I'd never done it in front of people before and it had always seemed to me more of a thing you'd do in private.

Anyway – that was the first shoot over and I was handed a cheque for two hundred pounds which aside from feeling a bit strange I was quite pleased to be receiving. It hadn't been a bad experience. Whether I'd liked it or not I couldn't be absolutely sure because the lights made me squint and part of me still thinks posing in that kind of way is a bit unseemly. But then that kind of misses the point. The thing about photography – like all 'art' – is that it needs to be seen.

It was when we'd finished that Tanya pointed out another possibility: that if I wanted to pursue it in a different direction – a little on-line publicity as she called it, she'd help me. That the pictures could feature as part of a text-message or something like that...I can't remember the exact words because though I have a computer, stuff like posting messages and texting is something I'd never been into. But it was when she pointed out how normal and commonplace that sort of thing is these days, particularly as a way of meeting people – and that if I wanted she would guide me through the basic procedure and help if I got stuck – that I started to listen.

Though I hadn't said anything at the time, the idea of a contacting someone (ie. a man) with a view to meeting him *did* appeal to me. Though I live alone and rarely see people it isn't because I don't want to. Deep down I'd like to meet people but I don't go to the places where people go, like pubs and clubs because I don't drink much and I'd stand out in those places and people would stare, and maybe comment, like at school. And I know that in those sort of places most men don't want to chat to fat women in that way, they prefer slimmer women. And if they didn't mind chatting up fat women they'd probably prefer to do it in private where people wouldn't see them.

Which is what made me think I might just go ahead; to put some of the pictures on-line and see what happened. For as long as I could remember I'd tended to shy away from people – to a point of seeing little beyond my own four walls sometimes for weeks on end. And the idea of meeting a man who I might get friendly with suddenly seemed an idea worth pursuing. I know I could have done what she was suggesting any time I'd wanted but doing the pictures encouraged me and gave me the idea to actually go ahead, particularly as they – or at least Tanya – had offered to help, which is half the battle: knowing there's help at hand if you get stuck.

It was the following night that I sat in front of my computer screen with notes I'd taken at Tanya's as to what to do. It's strange sitting in your own room, just you and a computer; a blank screen about to take you to places with little idea exactly where it will lead. In a way it's a bit scary – but in a way I guess it's supposed to be.

It took a bit of working out, clicking the right boxes and typing the right things and I had to knock at their door twice to ask about things I didn't understand but they didn't mind me asking and said they'd see me soon for the next 'shoot' and they'd got some interesting ideas, or Tanya had some interesting ideas, Hilary didn't say much at all.

Anyway – to cut a long story short – by the end of the evening I think I'd got somewhere and had managed to attach two of the earlier pictures Tanya had taken. I felt quite proud of myself which seemed the ideal point to leave it for now. I was tired but there was a sense of achievement, knowing that even as I closed the computer down, someone somewhere might, at that very minute, be looking at my pictures and thinking it might be a good idea to meet me. I'd often thought about men and dating but never seriously because it had never been part of my life nor was likely to be. But I guess that's one of the things about computers: that ultimately everything happens in private, without being watched or observed by anyone and meeting people can be a lot easier done that way, particularly if you're like me – overweight and not used to meeting people.

On arriving home from work the following day I went straight onto the computer, which is something I rarely do. Usually I either don't go on it at all or I wait till later.

I'd written down what to click so I wouldn't forget and I felt nervous about what might be about to appear on the screen. It was a bit of a let down when there was nothing – or nothing stemming from what I'd sent the previous night unless I'd clicked the wrong things. But then I reminded myself that these things take time and it might be a bit early; that people who answer these messages might go on computers later in the evening. So I left it there for the time being and went to make some tea.

It was after ten-o-clock when I tried again. Having waited a while would make it more interesting to see if anyone had answered my message. Even then it occurred to me that I didn't really know what to expect – or what I wanted or expected to happen; what kind of message I was likely to get. In a way it scared me, not in a sense of being frightened, but in a sense of not knowing exactly what might be about to turn up.

My heart leapt when I saw two messages had appeared on my screen. Deep down I'd still thought it was unlikely I'd get a reply; that I'd have done something wrong – clicked the wrong tab or failed to put the right information in, but there they were, as clear as on a tv screen. I actually leant closer to the screen to open the first message, which, at first glance – I didn't understand. Then I realised the man was just trying to be funny so I deleted it. Another one I didn't understand at all. I went back to where I'd put the entry the previous evening to check it and went back to the screen and the next thing I saw was a photograph. And then, right next to it – a short paragraph. I tapped in some things Tanya had told me about and then I went back to the message and read it.

It was a man. It was strange reading a message from someone without knowing who he was or where he was but knowing he was out there somewhere – waiting and wanting to speak to me! Saying he liked the pictures and maybe we could meet up. I read it again and then for a third time.

I thought about telling Tanya but then decided not to, I suppose because I wanted it to be my secret. There's something about contacting people on a computer that makes you want to keep it to yourself. I'd written down what to do next so I followed my instructions and fortunately it all seemed to click into place, which doesn't always happen. There was no phone number which didn't surprise me and to be honest I didn't want. I wouldn't want to give my phone number on-line as you never know who might get hold of it and speaking to people you've never met on the phone didn't really appeal. It seemed to me half the point is not having to do that.

What I did next was text the man back, checking with my notes and reading everything on the screen twice – feeling a bit like one of the women at work who seem to be texting people all day long.

I soon got the hang of it. What struck me was how easy it was. Although I'd never had reason to do it, I'd always imagined texting and messaging would be quite a complicated business to get into.

Anyway, a message came back with a suggestion we meet and a suggested meeting-point which was when I started feeling a bit nervous – taking that step from communicating on a screen to meeting face to face. He'd added a photo of himself, or of his face, and just seemed quite 'normal', slightly round-faced with no particularly distinguishing features, which was fine by me. Had he been younger or more handsome it would have seemed strange because you'd expect someone like that to look for someone who was prettier and slimmer and maybe meet them in public. Plus – I had the odd feeling that a 'normal' looking man would be easier to talk to. His face was a bit podgy which I quite liked. Maybe we had something in common!

I thought about the place he suggested meeting in – a pub a few miles from where I live, which *did* get me thinking seriously about what I might be letting myself in for. But then if I was going to have doubts every time I got an answer I'd be wasting my time and at the end of the day I needed to make a decision – either to go ahead with it or forget it.

I already knew what my decision would be. I knew I didn't want to leave it there. That I was being presented with an opportunity I might regret not pursuing – if only on the grounds of being too scared or too timid simply because it was all new to me.

On doing a bit of research getting to the place he'd suggested would mean catching a bus and possibly a cab but I didn't mind. The fact that the man had seen and presumably liked my pictures made me feel good about myself in a way I hadn't felt for a long time. He hadn't said anything about bringing any of the pictures but I'd decided I'd take a few of them so we could talk about them if he wanted to.

So – I decided to go ahead. Even though I still wasn't necessarily expecting anything to come of it, it would be nice to meet someone and talk. Plus – I was thinking about something else Tanya had said: that this was a way of meeting people designed for people like me: people who don't go to the sort of places where you meet people or haven't got time. And people who don't automatically, or easily, fit in; or *feel* they can fit in. Which I didn't mind her saying because it's true.

On the night I took a while thinking what to wear which I know is stupid, and makes me sound like one of those woman people make jokes about. Silly too because we tend to care more about what we wear than the people who see us, who often don't care *what* we're wearing, like at my sister's wedding last year. I wasn't sure about wearing make-up. I don't think I'd worn make-up in my entire life. But I'd have to admit that with the pictures at Tanya's it had helped – highlighting the bits that could do with a bit of highlighting was the way Tanya had put it. So I went ahead and used some of the make-up from the pictures, a little eye-liner and some blush on my cheeks but no lipstick; I'd always felt I'd look a bit silly wearing lip-stick, like I was just making up for being fat; trying to compensate for it or even hide the fact. I went for a dress but nothing too fancy. I didn't want to overdo it. Plus – if I'm honest, a dress helps hide my figure better than a skirt or jeans, not that I'd have worn jeans. I think it pays to make a bit of an effort.

So – at half-past seven I set off, closing the door behind me and pulling my coat tight round my shoulders. Getting to the place proved a bit more of a problem than I'd imagined with the bus not going a direct route and then the nearest cab firm being some way off.

But an hour or so after setting off – sitting in a taxi, brushing myself down for no reason other than I'd soon be getting out of the cab – I knew there was no turning back. That I'd made a promise to myself, that for good or bad, I needed to stick with. I was thinking about the man I was about to meet, a man about whom I knew nothing beyond in a picture on a screen – other than he was a bit podgy-looking and was happy to meet a woman who was even more podgy-looking.

The thing about going into pubs is not so much people looking at you as knowing someone was looking out for you and not knowing where they are or even *who* they are. Plus the odd sensation of eyeing people sitting on stools or in some cases at tables who routinely return the look. I'd always been aware of people looking at me though I'd long since come round to thinking it's more them imagining carrying my sort of weight around than looking in any disapproving way.

It was curiosity as much as anything guiding me past the first line of alcoves to a point where I thought I might have spotted him.

A man sitting alone whose looks and expression, even from a distance, were vaguely familiar. I looked again in his direction and on making eye contact offered a sort of smile to see if it got any response. He sort of smiled back, at which point I guessed it was him. I took the plunge – moving towards the table to make it seem I was meeting someone I already knew.

He said my name, phrasing it like a question and extending his hand. It felt odd like we were meeting for some purpose other than merely social. I was sure everyone in the pub knew exactly what was going on, drawing a halt to their conversations to follow our every move like they wanted to witness it first-hand.

I took a seat opposite, partly to avoid people's eyes. It took me a bit by surprise when he asked if I wanted a drink. I'm not a great drinker and had hardly thought about it, a lager and lime being the first idea to spring to mind. He was drinking beer and was soon back from the bar clutching a half pint glass and a pint glass.

They say pubs are useful meeting places and I could see there was something in that; the surroundings and dim light give a sense of privacy that isn't the same in other places.

I was interested to see what he looked like; much as expected from the picture though he was a bit rounder in the face, chubbier than I'd anticipated with bags under his eyes. I was a bit surprised and possibly a bit disappointed that he wasn't a bit bigger overall, as in...overweight, a bit more like me. He was largish but mostly round his middle. Like me he seemed a bit shy, not wanting to come across as over-confident, not quite sure what to say beyond establishing I'd got to the pub without too much of a problem.

We made the kind of conversation I suppose people make on first meetings: where we lived, our work, a bit of family stuff though neither of us had a great deal to say on that score. I'd expected it to be a bit hard-going and it struck me that Bernard didn't seem one for long drawn-out conversation, which was okay with me. Situations others slip into automatically can be quite a strain when you live alone. He seemed nice enough though I noticed he had a habit of looking away when he was speaking, like looking you directly in the eye was something he either preferred not to do or couldn't do. He worked for the Post-Office and lived in a flat a few miles from the town centre; circumstances that weren't hugely different from mine. He too led a fairly quiet life; not really one for socialising or partying. We obviously had a fair amount in common though you could never be sure how far that would stretch. I told him a bit more about myself: work, the flat. I wasn't sure whether to say anything about the photo-shoot thinking it might be best to leave that for now or at least until I showed him the pictures I'd brought and had in my bag.

We had two more drinks but three glasses of lager was enough for me. It's true that alcohol helps conversation and we managed to keep talking, sticking to simple topics like tv programmes and the kind of things we ate which seems a bit boring but when you live alone these things matter, as it's easy to get lazy when you're only cooking for yourself. Which was something he admitted to being – tending to over rely on take-aways like Chinese food or fish and chips. Out of politeness, neither of us mentioned weight issues. Though in my case it seemed strange *not* to talk about it, like I was pretending it wasn't an issue even though I was sitting opposite him. It crossed my mind whether eating-out was on his mind, not tonight but maybe in future. Whatever happened between us one of the things I *wouldn't* be doing was inviting him (or anyone) round my flat for a meal. I'd always hated the idea of cooking for others. We talked a bit about holidays though neither of us were too bothered about holidays in the usual sense.

At the end of the evening he offered to get me a cab to get me to the bus station, the idea being to stay in the cab to get him home which seemed to make sense so I agreed. He offered to let the cab take me all the way home but I said no because it would be out of his way and I wasn't sure I wanted him to know where I lived just yet.

I sat in the front of the cab which was probably a good

idea. When we got to the bus stop I got out and we reminded ourselves what we'd agreed before leaving the pub: to meet again, making it in nine days time so as not to have to go through all the arranging again. We'd make it the same pub which was fine by me. Though I'm not much of a drinker I can see that pubs are good places to go to talk.

I was quite relieved looking back on the evening. Meeting people, especially for the first time, can sometimes be awkward but it seemed to have gone okay. I wasn't building my hopes up about it leading to anything because it's best not to think in such terms when you first meet someone. Plus – a rather odd thought that really shouldn't matter – was that he seemed a little older than he was saying which I might have been wrong about or maybe he was sensitive about his age. I know some people are like that. I don't often think about it, partly because I'm still on the youngish side compared to most people. Plus – people in my position tend to have more pressing considerations.

I'd be lying if I said I didn't give Bernard any thought over the next few days. We'd agreed not to swap phone numbers. I don't like speaking on the phone and we agreed it wasn't really appropriate for us to be doing that. I wasn't love-struck or anything stupid like that. That sort of thing never really applied to me. But I *was* thinking that if things turned out okay, it might be nice to go places together; to have a kind of relationship though what kind of relationship would be impossible to predict and I wasn't thinking along those lines. It was best not to think about it too much, we'd only met once. But I don't mind admitting that snuggling up in bed that night was a bit more cosy than on other nights.

I often try to think of scenes or picture events to help me get to sleep and I was trying to picture Bernard's 'look'. I could see the sagging eyes like the man on tv who used to do dog-food adverts – a kind of ordinary 'look' which I actually quite liked.

Work went much the same as usual though seeing the girls in their breaks tapping into their phones left me curious about who they might be communicating with, like in a way I was close to being part of that scene myself now. I don't have one of those Smartphones, or whatever they're called, as I'd never had any need for one.

Once or twice I passed Tanya and Hilary in the corridor and they said 'hi'. They didn't ask about anything that had happened, probably thinking it was none of their business. Like I say, we all tend to mind our own business, particularly when it comes to things like that.

I was feeling a bit on edge the day of the second meeting with Bernard. Meeting him for the first time had been fairly casual, a kind of getting-to-know-him stage. Meeting again meant there could be more to it than that; that maybe it could be leading somewhere.

Though it still seemed stupid I spent quite a long time getting ready, trying on three dresses before I settled on a blue one with a matching top. I was getting quite a dab hand at putting make-up on. It was almost getting to feel like an everyday activity, reassuring to be doing the same things as other women.

On the walk to the bus stop I was thinking what I might have to drink. The lager and lime was okay but it was a bit sweet. I'd talked to the women at work about their drinking preferences and vodka and tonic or bitter lemon had been mentioned so I thought I might go for one of them. Nothing wrong in trying to seem a little sophisticated.

I was also thinking of things to talk about. When you rarely meet people or rarely talk to people making conversation isn't so straightforward. I knew the key was to think of subjects that were neither too trivial nor too serious. A possibility was my CD's. I like the male singers like Neil Sedaka and Roy Orbison. Or the tv we liked. I liked watching the dramas and some music programmes. There's always sport and politics but I'm not into sport at all, not surprisingly. And don't know much about politics. Bernard gave me the impression he might be the same, so we probably had something in common there. I wondered if he was a cinema-goer or into the theatre. I wasn't really into either but it didn't seem wise to shut out all possible lines of conversation for no obvious reason.

Knowing where I was going and how to get there made it easier and I didn't have to wait long for a cab. They let me sit in the office which was warmer. It was odd listening to the man behind the desk, who was Asian, talking to people on the phone sometimes in his own language, sometimes in English, and sometimes a mixture. Whilst I was waiting I sorted through the pictures I'd brought. We'd talked a bit about the pictures last time and when I'd said I could bring a few more he seemed to approve, which was quite reassuring to hear. When you're like me you tend to assume your appearance will either get a negative reaction or no reaction, though I suppose with Bernard that was never likely to be the case considering he'd seen the pictures before meeting me. Maybe we could talk a bit about them. I couldn't see any reason for not doing that since he was likely of a similar opinion; that there was no shame in depicting the female form – in whatever shape or size.

I felt more comfortable entering the pub knowing who I was meeting, making me feel like one of thousands of people for whom entering pubs is neither here nor there.

Bernard was in the same seat as before and he rose from his seat as I made my way over to the table which seemed quite an old-fashioned thing to do, like he was making an attempt to be ultra-polite. He extended his hand and we shook hands which, in a way, seemed strange, but it would have been odd not to greet each other and kissing on the cheek would hardly have been appropriate, certainly not yet.

I felt quite sophisticated saying 'vodka and tonic' when he asked what I wanted to drink, like a regular drinker who knew about these things.

Meeting people the second time round is in some ways easier because you know a bit about each other and the most difficult bit is behind you. Which didn't detract from the fact that engaging in conversation isn't always as easy as people imagine, particularly with Bernard giving little impression of wanting to make it easy for either of us. He'd seemed that way inclined all along – but particularly now, on the second occasion. Lapses in conversation are fine but can become a bit awkward when you both know that isn't the reason for being there. We talked about what we'd been doing since we last met which, in my case, wasn't a great deal, but with me that'd the way it is most days of the week.

He told me about an incident at work where there'd been a complaint about a parcel and one of his colleagues had been accused of mislaying it which, in the Post Office, was quite a serious issue. Understandably so if it was a valuable parcel like a birthday or Christmas gift. He wasn't directly involved but he knew the man charged and he'd been disciplined. We talked a bit about the post system but not much. There isn't a lot to say about things you're not directly involved in. Bernard said there was talk of putting it up for privatisation but he didn't say much which was probably a good thing. I'm not too well up with politics and he didn't appear to be too interested, viewing it more as something to say. I noticed his habit of looking away when he was talking was still there. I wondered if it was because he was shy or worried about something. I'd also noticed he had a mole under his chin but I can't think it was the sort of thing he'd be too self-conscious about. He'd also said nothing about his family and I wasn't inclined to ask. You never know what the circumstances might be and that it might be a sensitive area. I didn't have much to say on the subject. My father's dead and my mother lives in a home. I have an older sister who got married last year. I see her from time to time but not very often.

There were moments when nothing much was said, which I actually didn't mind, though I didn't want him being the one to have to break the silences. I know some people – the women at work for example – never allow breaks in conversation. But sometimes it's nice to take in the surroundings without needing to talk. The pub was busier than before and I noticed the other bar, the restaurant bit was a lot busier.

I was getting the impression Bernard was definitely shy which wasn't any great surprise. I think people who meet like we did are often shy which is what leads them to do it that way. I'm the same. Even at school I didn't used to mix a lot with the other children. At comprehensive I had a friend Kim and we used to go to the library sometimes or just sit in a classroom and talk over our packed-lunch.

I noticed Bernard liked to observe what was going on around but I also noticed that when my attention was elsewhere he would make a point of looking at me, which was odd in that when he was actually talking to me he would often look away. But I didn't mind because I think it comes from being self-conscious. Plus, I didn't actually mind him looking at me. It wasn't something I found displeasing. I think we all hesitate to say things when we can sometimes show our feelings in other ways.

He asked about the pictures which reminded me that I'd brought some with me and had them in my bag. I wasn't worried about letting him see them because that was, after all, what had led to us meeting in the first place. And we'd already talked a bit about the pictures and how the lighting had been arranged to produce the best effect.

I showed him some of the ones where my dress was hitched up to reveal an expanse of thigh, two of which had one of my boobs partly exposed and cupped in my hand though it was in the shadow of the top part of my dress so you couldn't see it entirely, which I think was the point of the picture though I didn't bother saying anything about that. Following what we'd said about lighting and its effects it would be pretty much stating the obvious. I didn't give these things a great deal of thought myself now.

We'd got to the point where another round of drinks was

due which I offered to buy because so far I hadn't bought any drinks and I'm not one of those women who see themselves as incapable of going to the bar. Also it would allow him to look at the pictures without me watching or waiting for him to say something complimentary.

He didn't actually say anything about the pictures when I returned to the table. I put the two drinks down and settled into my seat, expecting him to offer some comment but he didn't. I had two more pictures which I could show him later but he didn't seem too interested. It struck me that viewing pictures on his computer could simply be a route to meeting people. Which again I had no problem with. I understand that one of the reasons for viewing people on-line is to get an impression of the person behind the picture. Which was what I was doing too, so it was fair enough.

To change the subject, I asked about what music he liked. He said he didn't listen to music much but if he did it tended to be stuff from the sixties or seventies: The Beatles or some of the black soul singers. I told him my favourites were Neil Sedaka and Roy Orbison. When he asked why, I wasn't really sure. It's strange with music. I don't listen to a lot of it but sometimes you hear something that just seems to grab you. Why...you can't always say. With me it was *You Got It* by Roy Orbison but I couldn't really say why other than it was catchy.

I realised I needed to go to the loo so I thought it might be an idea to leave the pictures on the table so he could browse through them whilst I was away. I still wasn't sure he was that interested but maybe having me sitting opposite him whilst he was looking at them didn't help.

Like last time I was aware how a few drinks can help in these situations; when you're not used to making conversation but find yourself able to open up a little. When I got back I told him about some of the places I'd lived in and the trouble I'd had in the past finding a suitable place. How it isn't easy with the cost of renting and landlords who don't always know, or care much, about some of their properties. I talked a bit about work and how they'd set up a 'management training scheme' that one or two had suggested I might go for even though I'd never been sure whether I really want to go down that line, that it sometimes seemed more hassle than it was likely worth.

Back to the pictures. I suddenly felt bold enough to explain how one or two of them were done; how the lighting was arranged to leave part of the top half of me in shadow including part of my face. The point – as Tanya had put it – not being so much to show an individual's features, as to present an image for the eye to work on, which is the point behind a lot of this kind of photography; that it isn't what you *see* as much as what you don't see or *imagine* you're seeing.

Which was when it struck me he was barely listening; that what I was saying was either way over his head or simply boring him, going into detail about things he might not be too interested in.

Which, as it turned out – wasn't quite the case.......

It was picking up on the general drift of what I was saying that he leant into the table – a quick glance over each shoulder indication that what was about to be said would be best kept between the two of us. Then looking me in the eye to let me know, in no uncertain terms, that he...'liked a bit of meat on a woman'.

Then quickly back to his former pose – prepared to have the conversation pick up as and when seemed fitting.

I can't remember *how* or *if* I reacted. Or whether I was supposed *to* react.

Not that it would have made a great deal of difference. Here was a man whose awkwardness and self-consciousness were already shaping into something deeper.

Evidence of which was leaning forward once again, telling me how he...'liked something to grab hold of. And adding – lest there should be any doubt as to how I fitted into the picture – that if I were to stick around long enough, I'd likely find out exactly what he meant!

I suppose it's easy to misread situations. To put difficulties engaging with people down to factors that can't easily be explained. In Bernard's case – the realisation that everything we'd been talking about since first setting eyes on each other: work, where we lived, the tv we watched, had been simply marking time; time that had finally run its course – on both sides of the table.

It was on rising from my seat and reaching for my bag that I was aware of him following my movements, still giving the impression he was hopeful of getting some kind of a response.

Once outside, having had chance to breathe the air and put a bit of distance between us, I was aware it was getting late and that I needed to give some thought as to how I was actually going to get home. Which I knew inevitably meant returning to the pub in order to phone a cab.

I knew there were two bars and that I could enter by a different door, go straight up to the bar-staff, explain I'd been there earlier and could they get me a cab and then wait in the next bar to where we'd been sitting. Even if Bernard were to see me my guess was he'd keep his distance. And if he didn't, help would be at hand.

Half reassured I headed for the door at the near side, the pub's busier side.

It was still busy. I approached the part of the bar where a man was washing glasses, explaining I'd been there earlier and now realised I needed to get a taxi. He went to speak to someone and said he'd give me a number. I needed to use the bar phone but it wasn't a problem and the taxi said it would come but it would be at least twenty minutes, which I said was okay.

It felt strange being in the same pub but standing in a different bar – doing my best to blend in with surroundings that only twenty minutes ago I'd been a part of. Aware how quickly circumstances can change. That I was now amongst 'normal' people who knew each other, who were totally at home in each other's company and whose evenings would end in much the same vein as they had started.

I ordered a mineral water and moved to occupy a space at the end of the bar so as not to be in anyone's way.

The bar we'd been in was within vision but only by leaning to peer through a mass of bodies.

It was a few minutes later that an opportunity arose – a gap appearing between the line of bottles and the bar itself.

Bernard was still there, glass in hand – staring into space as if the events of the past twenty minutes or so were somehow entirely beyond him.

Which – at the time and on reflection – I think was likely the case. That what was done was done. That there'd be no looking back, no revisiting the scene. That another day meant other overweight woman popping up on a computer screen; a woman appearing to tick all the boxes for someone on the lookout for 'something a little different'. And who was ready with the kind of offer she'd likely find hard to refuse.

The cab would be another ten, maybe fifteen minutes. Which meant I had a choice: either stay in the bar or stand outside. It wasn't raining and it would be easier to be spotted if I stood outside.

Pulling the door to, I looked for somewhere to stand: a spot over by the window of the neighbouring bar as good a spot as any – semi-illuminated by a light fixed into the wall above the window.

I checked with my watch. The cab might be longer than they'd said but it didn't really matter; it was ordered and at some point would arrive. It wasn't unreasonable to expect delays ordering a cab at this time of night.

It was a decent enough spot, allowing me to keep an eye out for passing vehicles whilst keeping an eye on both in and outside the bar.

Until, around twenty minutes later, a pair of headlights appeared followed by a car with the 'taxi' sign showing on its roof, eventually drawing to a halt a few yards away, the driver stopping to call my name through the passenger window.

On the way home I was reminded of Tanya's line about the human form meaning different things to different people. With time to reflect on how right she'd been.

The following day I'd tell her that the second shoot wasn't going to happen. It wasn't that I was against the idea but maybe at the end of the day, posing in front of a camera like that just wasn't my cup of tea.

If it meant a return to solitary days and solitary nights then so be it. I'd long since been of the opinion there are far worse ways of passing time. After all – the only shame in the shape and size of a person's appearance is in the minds of people choosing to see it that way.

* * * * *

.